Bob Moats

I0567257

Dominatrix Murders

By Bob Moats

New Edits as of Sept 03, 2012

REV-0326141630

1

Dominatrix Murders

This book is licensed for your personal use only. This book may not be re-sold or given away to other people. If you would like to share this book with another person, please purchase an additional copy for each recipient. If you're reading this book and did not purchase it, or it was not purchased for your use only, please purchase your own copy. Thank you for respecting the hard work of this author.

This is a work of pure fiction. Names, characters, places, and incidents either are the product of the author's imagination or are used fictitiously, and any resemblance to actual persons, living or dead, business establishments, events, or locales is entirely coincidental.

ISBN – 978-0-9960634-4-9

For information and address:
Magic 1 Productions
P.O. Box 524, Fraser MI 48026-0524
Website: http://murdernovels.com
Cover design by Bob Moats
Photo www.fotosearch.com Stock Photography

Bob Moats

Other Jim Richards series books by Bob Moats

For a preview or to purchase a book, go to
http://murdernovels.com

What a few people are saying about Murder Novels by Bob Moats

Mr. Moats, I just got your novel "Classmate Murders" and have to let you know, I read it in one evening. That is the first book I have ever done that with. That was the most enjoyable book I have ever read. I just started reading e-books, and reading again, after getting my wife a Kindle. This book was my 12th, and the best. I just got Las Vegas Showgirls to (read) tomorrow evening. I look forward to reading many of your books in this series. I have been searching for an author and books that were fun, entertaining reads. Your books are just the ticket.

Regards, A new fan, Bill from South Carolina

****

Another very nice comment submitted through my website from Micki P.:

"I recently was given a kindle for my 60th birthday. The first book I downloaded was the Classmate Murders and have now read every one of the them. Today I started on the Fatal Rejection series. Thank you for the wonderful ride with Jim and Penny and all the rest of the troop. I have laughed and giggled thru the stories, my poor family gave me the strangest looks! Now I really want a little Yorkie!! Fatal Rejection so far is another great read! I

4

will be looking out for more of Jim Richards and since you are my #1 Author, anything of yours I can find."

Special thanks to:

To my new editor Sally Berneathy who under took the task of going through the most recent copy of this book and giving it the edits it has been needing. Hopefully now it is better. If you need a great editor for your book go to http://www.sallyberneathy.com and check her out.

Thank you for purchasing this book, I hope you enjoy it as much as I enjoyed writing them for my faithful readers. Please feel free to email me to tell me what you thought about my stories. I can be reached through http://murdernovels.com thanks again!

The Jim Richards Family of Readers is listed in the back of the book.

Dominatrix Murders
By Bob Moats

Chapter One

The paint hadn't even dried yet on the door lettering when she opened the door and stood admiring the name, "Jim Richards, Private Investigations." She looked to me, gave me a million dollar smile, and slinked to the chair at my desk where she seated herself, slowly crossing a pair of legs that screamed, lick me. She flipped back a shock of blonde hair from her gorgeous face and looked at me with eyes so deep, I was lost in them, then she called my name.

"Mr. Richards," she said in a sultry voice, then paused. Then said again, "Mr. Richards, I want my husband killed."

I suddenly came out of my daydream, staring at a frumpily dressed, middle-aged, mousy, brown-haired woman who stared back at me through glasses thick as bottle bottoms. I said, "Excuse me, you want your husband killed?"

"What? Oh, my goodness, no! I said I want him tailed, or followed, whatever you P.I.s call it," she exclaimed.

"Ah, I'm sorry, I'm a bit jet lagged from a flight back from Las Vegas," I lied.

It had been about five weeks since we got back from Vegas, and I spent the first week helping Deacon and Lynn pack his belongings to move back to Vegas. I would miss him. We had become good friends when we met during the classmate murders. He had been the cop assigned as protection for Penny, my girlfriend. Now he was really happy being with Lynn, the detective he met and fell in love with in Las Vegas. I wished him well. I also envied the hell out of him for moving to Vegas.

As soon as we got back to Detroit, Penny helped me find an office to work my P.I. business out of, got it supplied and I opened up shop. I still had a good deal of money left over from the check Penny's TV station gave me for working as her bodyguard in Vegas, so I was able to advertise and wait for the clients to come streaming in. After about a week of no streaming, Mrs. Flagg was my first customer, not the sexy blonde needing protection from a crazed stalker, just a quiet housewife needing closure.

"OK, why do you want me to follow him?" I asked, figuring he was probably trying to stay away from her.

"I think he's having an affair. He's not himself anymore, distant from me, not as affectionate as he used to be," she said. She teared up, so I moved a box of tissues over to her. She took one and thanked me.

She continued, "We've been married for almost three years, and they have been good years, but in the last few months, Ralph, that's his name, has started to act different."

"How so?" I asked.

"Well, our sex activities have diminished to a point where we only do it once every other day. It used to be a daily affair." She smiled.

I didn't really want to hear that, imagining having sex with this woman. I asked, "Do you feel he is cheating on you?"

"I don't know, but yesterday I was going to do laundry and was gathering his clothes. I saw his gym bag and checked it and found a pair of leather shorts, something he's never shown me before. I don't know what to make of it, but I sense he may be straying." She looked away from me, as though wanting to say more.

8

"Is there more you want to say, Mrs. Flagg?" I asked.

"Please call me Elma," she offered. Then paused, thinking of how she wanted to continue.

"Well, our love making has gotten a bit more, well, rough. He has been wanting me to tie him to the bed lately, and asking me to do things to him I've never done before. Spanking, things like that," she said and went quiet.

My brain was slowly melting from the image of being in bed with this woman. "Well, if I could get some information from you, I can do a cursory investigation to see if there is more to his strange behavior." I worded my intentions carefully.

"I just want him followed for a few days to see what he's been up to. He has been away from home a lot lately, which is why our sex has diminished. He comes home acting happy and then he just goes to bed. It's not like him."

"OK, write down everything I need to know about him, full name, address, place of work, gym he may go to, things like that." I handed her a pad and pencil and she started to write. After about ten minutes, she handed me a full page of more info than I needed, but it might help. I handed her a printed list of my charges. "Now, this card has my fees on it. You decide how you want me to handle this, and that will be my charge."

Dominatrix Murders

She looked at the card and said the full investigation would be fine, she had money to spend, and she was rather wealthy. She took out a wad of cash, peeled off a couple of hundred dollar bills, and set them on my desk. "Here's the advance," she said.

I said I thought I had all the information I needed and would be in touch with her in a few days with anything I could find. She reached into her purse and pulled out a wallet size picture of a very handsome man, handed it to me and said it was her husband. I asked if I could keep it, and she said yes. I was marveling at how this good-looking guy could have hooked up with this woman, but she said she was rich, could be a reason for marriage. She thanked me and left.

I sat back in my creaky desk chair, mulling over what Ralph could be up to. Leather pants, rough sex, spanking, sounds like the boy was getting into kink. I looked at the paper she wrote out for me, down the list of places he frequented, then back to the picture again. I was feeling like this woman might be in for a big disappointment.

My door opened again and I looked up hoping it was the sultry blonde. Unfortunately it was Trapper. He looked at the new door lettering, then looked around my tiny, and empty, office and said, "Well, I was expecting a room full of angry wives looking to catch their husbands in flagrant activities." He grinned.

"Only one so far, and she just left," I lamented.

"Talking about that near blind woman who almost ran into me?" He grinned.

"Yep, husband is now into leather shorts and rough sex."

"Sex with her, eww." He shivered.

I showed him the picture and said, "Yeah, imagine that and him."

"What's she got, money or a hot body under all those baggy clothes?"

"Money, she says she's got enough to afford me." I laughed.

"Getting many clients yet?" he asked.

"She's the first. Hope it isn't going to be this slow starting off."

"Well, if it helps, I can send a few customers your way. We get a number of housewives who all think their husbands are cheating on them. We tell them it's not a crime to stray, so we can't help them. I'll be sure to let them know you're available," he said.

Dominatrix Murders

"I appreciate that. Have you heard anything from Deacon?" I wondered.

"I got a call from my old buddy Weber, asking if I recommended him for a job in Vegas Metro police. I said that he was the laziest, most incompetent goof off I ever had on my squad, but he'd be crazy not to hire him." He smiled.

"You did know he was faking that limp from his hip?" I asked.

"Of course I did. I saw him dancing around the squad room one day. I was going to call him on it, but what the hell, he deserved a little time off."

I had grown to like Trapper. As a cop he was good, as a person he was better.

"If it helps, I know a couple of lawyers who occasionally need a P.I. to do some leg work for them. Interested?" he asked.

"I'm not crazy about lawyers, but I wouldn't turn the work down," I replied.

"That's good, because I have a lawyer friend who has a touchy case that he needs some evidence gathered. It's out of my jurisdiction, and he doesn't want to involve cops elsewhere. Interested?"

"If you do me a favor, I might be." I grinned.

"Do I have to kill anyone?" He smiled.

"Nope, just run a background check on Medusa's husband," I requested.

He laughed and said, "Deal." He took a card out of his jacket and handed it to me. "Mark said to call him, if you take the case."

"You were sure of yourself, weren't you?" I said.

He looked around the empty room and said it was a good bet. I made a copy of Flagg's info and gave it to him.

"It seems every P.I. on TV or in books has a cop on the inside. Looks like I'm yours," he said with a wink.

"Oh, well, I start at the bottom and work my way up." I grinned.

He laughed and headed for the door. "Remember, this isn't Las Vegas. There's no glamour here."

I said I was going to put up flashing lights around my door to make me feel like I was still in Vegas. He smiled and went out the door without saying good-bye. He did that a lot. I sat for a moment looking at my door, trying to remember where I put that flashing light rope from Christmas. What the hell, I just might do it.

*

Chapter Two

I called Mark Benson, attorney at law, and introduced myself. I said that Will Trapper said he might need some help with a case. Mark thanked me for calling and asked if I could come to his office tomorrow so he could show me what he needed. I said I could make it. We agreed on 1 p.m., and I said I'd be there. I hung up, put the appointment in my Palm, and then looked at Ralph Flagg's information again, wondering where to start. I decided to see what Trapper came up with on the background check before I ventured out. I straightened my office for the hundredth time, and decided to call it a day.

My office was in a small professional building in Fraser that had cheap rent. Otherwise, it would be more than half-empty. I went out to my faithful '89 Crown Vic and drove up Garfield Road to 15 mile Road, and then out to Jefferson Avenue. I pulled into Penny's drive and parked on the side of the garage, then went in but didn't see Penny right away. I called to her. No answer. I went to the back enclosed porch and looked out. I could see her sitting on the small boat dock for a boat we didn't have. I walked down to the water and she turned to me and smiled.

"Hi, sweetie, home from a hard day investigating?" she said. I sat next to her.

"Yep, I racked my brain trying to come up with things to do. I played about 30 Sudoku games on my Palm. I'm up to twenty minutes per puzzle now." I grinned. "But I do have two cases now," I said proudly.

"Wow, what adventures are you going on?" She beamed. "Murder, kidnapping, drugs, or chasing bad husbands?"

"Chasing a husband in leather shorts," I replied. She looked puzzled. I explained my visit with Elma Flagg, Ralph's wife. Then I told her about Trapper throwing a case my way for a lawyer friend of his.

"Ah, a lawyer. You really going to take it?" she said, knowing I disliked them.

"It's a paying gig, so I'll put up with it. How was your show today?" I asked.

"I had two women on who were teaching wives to spice up their marriage with a little bondage and some light S&M." She grinned.

Dominatrix Murders

I stared for a second and said, "You're kidding? Did you TiVo it so I can see it?"

"Yes, I did, as you know I do every day, Mr. Smart P.I. Why? Are you into bondage now?"

"Well, as I said, my client thinks her husband is getting into some weird areas now, so I need to be informed about the subject," I explained. "Did they talk leather and whips?"

"You'll have to watch the show to see, I'm not going to explain things twice to you." She smiled.

"What ever happened to that stripper pole you wanted for the house?" I asked, changing the subject.

She just smiled and said, "It's on order. I'm going to book a stripper on the show who teaches women to work the pole for exercise and the fun of it."

"Or profit. You could start a nice little sideline entertaining gentleman callers," I said.

She ignored me and continued, "The show is getting a stripper pole for the demo and I claimed it after they're done with it. My producer said only if he could come and watch. So, I'm selling tickets."

"$20 for men at the door, plus nice tips. We'll make a killing." I grinned.

"What do you mean, we?" she said.

We talked a bit more, then I helped her up and we went in the house. I went out to the family room to get the TiVo ready to watch the show, and Penny said she was going to throw some grilled cheese on the stove. I said that was fine with me. I sat waiting for Penny before starting the show, which was now being picked up by the CW network, running mornings around 11 a.m. Penny was pleased with the reaction she was getting from the ratings. She was getting more controversial guests and subjects to keep up the interest. I hoped all the weirdness didn't rub off on her. She brought me two grilled cheese, two beers for both of us, and we sat and watched her show. She never really liked to watch herself on TV, but since the show went nationwide, she wanted to watch for things that needed improvement.

The show opened with the new format, no longer showing Penny around Detroit. The show had to be more generic. It had some nice pictures of her in front of places she's never been to, thanks to the wonders of special effects. She came on the TV and said, "Welcome world, I'm Penny Wickens, and this is *Penny for your Thoughts*." At least they kept her show name. She announced that today's show dealt with spicing up your marriage with a little leather and lace, also known as bondage and S&M. She introduced her guests today, Mistress Terry and Mistress Dyan. They both wore the traditional black leather bustiers, choke collars, spiked heels and mesh nylons, but Mistress Dyan was wearing a cat-woman mask. She said she was a single Mom and was protecting her identity.

"Single moms of the world rise up and snap your whips." I smirked. Penny whacked me. "Sorry," I offered.

We watched the show as the two women explained a little about SMBD and the beneficial effects on a marriage if practiced properly. I wondered if Ralph had watched this show. Or Elma. They went into various paraphernalia for hog tying your man and some simple whips and paddles for stimulating his libido. I was just about covering my eyes over the toys they had. I looked at Penny and hoped she didn't get any ideas. She glanced sideways at me, smiled and made a strange little growl. I just said, "Forget it."

She laughed when it ended, and said I should have no fear of being handcuffed in the night, although the thought was intriguing. It was 9 p.m. and we had been watching TV for a while when the phone rang. I answered.

"Hello?"

"Is this the famous Fearless Fosdick?" came a male voice.

I said, "I am," and asked, "Is this the famous Dick Tracy?"

I heard Lynn's voice saying she was and that Deacon was with her on the speakerphone. I waved Penny over, and she came.

"How the hell are you two doing?" I asked, holding the phone so Penny could hear.

Deacon was talking. "Great. We're all settled in, and I'm on the Metro squad now. They put me in Detectives because of my natural abilities."

Lynn interjected, " Bull hockey. I kissed a lot of ass to get him on. Don't let him fool you."

"How's things in Michigan?" Deacon asked.

"Same crappy weather, same lousy economy, same high unemployment, otherwise really good," I joked.

They both laughed, and Lynn said, "Penny, I've been watching your show every morning at work, I lock myself away and watch it. You are really good at it."

Penny blushed and said, "Thank you, but most of it is special effects."

Lynn and Deacon sounded happy, and we talked a while longer about what was going on in our little worlds. I told Deacon about Trapper helping me with my cases now. He said he was going to call him tonight to say thanks for the praise he gave Weber. I told both of them we missed them, and Penny said we'd be out next summer for a vacation so they should be prepared for more murder and mayhem when we got there.

We said our good-byes and hung up. I looked at Penny. She had a sad look on her face. "What's wrong?" I asked.

"I just miss them, and the fun we had in Vegas," she said.

"Fun? I was nearly thrown off the tallest building on the west coast, you were almost kidnapped, I was shot in the chest and you nearly killed Nick North with my gun. That was fun?" I was amazed.

"Yes, it was. I miss it now we are back in boring Michigan."

"OK, I'll try and stir up a little murder and mayhem for you here. Just give me a week or two." I laughed.

We watched a little more TV, I got on the computer and checked my emails, remembering the ones from the classmate murders, or I should call it, the cheerleader murders. I had nothing important, so I got off and grabbed my girl's hand and pulled her to the bedroom, saying that I saw a couple of things on her show we might try. She asked if I had my handcuffs. I pulled them out of my back pocket and she laughed.

The next morning the phone rang. I answered.

"Still in bed? It's time to get to work," came a voice.

I asked, "Who the hell is this?"

"It's Trapper. I got some hot info for you, if you're working today." He sounded excited.

"I'll be in around 9, my usual time to start," I moaned.

He said he'd be there and hung up.

I looked at Penny and asked if she knew where the damn keys for the handcuffs were. I held up my hands, still cuffed together. She just laughed.

*

Chapter Three

We found the keys, but Penny insisted on teasing me a bit longer before I was extricated from the cuffs. I got ready and was on my way out after seeing Penny off to her show. It was taped around 9 a.m. for broadcast at 11 a.m. on the east coast and rebroadcast same time on the west coast, three hours later from here. I got to my office and found Trapper sitting on a chair in the lobby waiting for me.

"About time you got to work." He smiled.

I looked at my watch. It was just 8:40. I said, "Trapper, do you have any concept of time?"

He grinned. "You'll need my info for your investigation into your little pervert and possible murderer." He was glowing. "I want in on this bust if you get him."

I was puzzled. I opened up my office and we went in. Trapper planted himself in the client chair at my desk. I sat in my creaky desk chair and looked at him. "OK, what's so exciting?"

"I ran the background check on Mr. Wonderful and came up with some interesting facts. First, he's been married two times prior to Elma, both rich women. They both died mysterious deaths. Wife number one died in a car crash, no links to hubby, he was out of the country. Wife number two commits suicide by hanging. Hubby is out with drinking buddies the night in question. I ran a check on his driver's violations. He had three tickets for illegal parking in Pontiac in the last two months, all on the same street. I called a friend of mine on Pontiac PD and asked about the street in question. It has a party store, gas station, three ordinary houses and one huge mansion that houses a legal and above board bondage club. Coincidence? I think not." He took a breath.

"I think I should be watching Elma, not Ralph. Did he inherit the money from his first two wives?"

"Well, he lived high on the hog as they say, and most the money was gone by the time of the wives' deaths. Sounds like a quickie divorce to me, once the money dried up." He grinned.

I looked at Trapper and said, "If Elma dies mysteriously; I'm going to feel really bad that we didn't do something. But what can we do?"

"Well, he's been cleared of both his late wives' deaths, so we can't bring him in on that. I guess you'll have to tail him and see what he is up to. It might make him nervous if you were a little obvious about it," Trapper said.

"Yea, but he might take it out on Elma. She's not exactly Cindy Crawford, but she is a human being. I don't want to see her hurt," I said.

"Well, then you may just have to confide in her and ask her to hide out from him till you get something on him. Think she'd go for that?"

Dominatrix Murders

"I don't know. She enjoyed the sex he provided her. She may not give him up fast. You know the 'bad boy' syndrome," I said.

"Jimmy, being a detective creates many problems that you have to work out, which one is the most appealing and the one that gets nobody killed. Now you have to do the leg work to find out more about your bad boy." Trapper smiled. "Please keep me informed, not in an official capacity, but just curiosity on my part."

Trapper took a folded sheet of paper out of his inner coat pocket and dropped it in front of me. "This is the rest of his background check. Military, he was a combat medic. Financial, of course, he's got money, or Elma does. Criminal record, none. He's been a good boy," Trapper finished.

"Yea, the perfectly nice man next door who happens to be a wife killer," I said.

Trapper got up. "I heard from my friend Mark that you're taking his case."

"I'm going to see what he's got today, and I'll decide then," I said.

Trapper headed to the door, "Well, keep me in the loop, I'll see what I can stir up on the perfect husband." He smiled and went out the door.

I looked at the report Trapper gave me and thought about how I was going to attack this. I could bring in Elma and tell her my suspicions, but I really didn't have much to go on. So I would have to follow him for a couple days to see what he was up to. Elma still had money so he probably wouldn't harm her yet.

My door opened, and I looked up, finally into the bluest eyes on any gorgeous blonde I have ever seen. She smiled and asked where the Davis Travel Agency was. I was crushed, but told her upstairs. She went out. OK, I came so close. Not that I would cheat on Penny, not in a million years. She was all I could ever want or handle, but just having a sexy femme fatale as a client would have made me feel like I arrived in the world of P.I., kind of a Sam Spade thing.

Around noon, I went to get a bite to eat at my favorite place, Subway. I was watching the people around me wondering how many of them could be killers or closet perverts. I was cynical about people. I believe that 80 percent of people are basically stupid, 18 percent are trying to get what they can from the first 80, and the last 2 percent just didn't give a damn about the other 98. I was in the 2 percent. Not that I don't totally care about people. I do care about things. I just don't want to have to put up with stupid and conniving people. As a detective, I would try to cut through the bull and get some justice for those in need.

Dominatrix Murders

I was at Mark Benson's office building in Roseville at 1 p.m. and entered the very expensive looking layout that screamed big lawyer fees. I was asked by the receptionist who I wanted to see. I told her. She got on her phone and made a short call, smiled and sent me through a door to his private office.

"Mr. Richards, thank you for coming in. Have a seat." The shark smiled. "Will has told me good things about you."

"Well, he has a tendency to gloss over things," I said. "What kind of law are you into?" Jumping right in.

"This office handles both divorce and criminal," he said.

"Aren't they both the same?" I joked.

He laughed and said he'd have to remember that.

"What do you have for me? Will said you needed some evidence gathered?" I asked.

"Yes, I have a case of murder. My client, David Weston, says he was with a woman on the night his wife was murdered at their home here in Roseville, but we can't seem to find the woman to establish his alibi."

Bob Moats

I had read about the murders in the papers. I was a bit familiar with the facts but wanted to hear this lawyer's slant on it.

He pulled a file folder from his cabinet and handed it to me. "This is all the info on the case that I could get from him. I don't disbelieve him, but the circumstances are a little shaky."

"Was she a hooker or a happy home wrecker?" I inquired.

"My client says he met her in a bar in Mt. Clemens, they hit it off and ended up in a motel down off Groesbeck Highway in Fraser. The motel has a record of his renting the room, but the desk clerk doesn't remember any woman with him. Roseville police figured he rented the room to try to set up an alibi, and then knocked off his wife."

"Did the police sweep the room?" I asked.

"The room was cleaned by the maid by the time forensics got there. Bed sheets were changed and washed so any evidence was destroyed."

"Is your client out on bail or still in jail?"

"The judge denied him bail for the gruesomeness of the killing. His wife was hacked and decapitated. The judge wasn't sympathetic."

Dominatrix Murders

"I'll need to talk to Weston. Can you arrange it?" I asked.

"Sure, I'll call the county jail and get it set up. So, I presume you are taking the case?" He smiled.

I pulled out my rate card and handed it to him, "Only if you can afford me. This case would take the number 10 special, my most expensive rate."

He laughed and said, "I think I can afford it. You want a retainer advance?" I said I did, he got on his phone and told someone to cut a check and have it to the receptionist ASAP.

"Can I call you if I have further questions?" I asked.

He handed me his card after writing his cell phone number on it. "Call anytime, this case goes to trial in a week, and I have very little to go on. I'm counting on you."

I said, "I'll give you my first rate investigation." I smiled and got up. He rose, and we shook hands. I went out the door, picked up my check from the girl at the front desk and left the building.

I finally looked at the check once I was sitting in my car and just grinned.

*

Chapter Four

I drove back to my office to organize my attacks on the Weston case and Elma's. I was going to give priority to the lawyer because the case was coming up next week and I had little to go on. I didn't think Ralph would do any harm to Elma yet, and I could follow him in between checking on my murder case.

There was no blonde sitting in my lobby waiting for me. Instead Buck was sprawled out on a chair with his eyes closed. I flicked his nose, and he came alive, ready to fight. I stepped back and yelled that it was me.

He calmed and said, "Hey, Jimmy, what's happening?"

"How long have you been camped out here?" I asked.

"Only about a half hour. I just came by to see if you were still alive."

I opened the door, and he went for the client chair. I told him about my meetings with Elma and Trapper, then about the lawyer.

Dominatrix Murders

"Yah, I read about that Weston murder. Husband claims he was screwing some woman while his wife was being hacked up," he said.

"Yes, Buck, that about sums it up. I've been hired to find the mystery woman."

"While you find her, I can follow the kinky husband around," he said.

"I'm sure he'd notice someone as big as you tailing him. I'll find something better for you to do. Like intimidate witnesses who may have seen my supposed murderer and his pick-up on the night in question."

"Ya, I can rough them up." He smiled.

"No, just look scary." I laughed.

"I can't have any fun?" he lamented.

"Scary is fun." I smiled. He agreed.

"So, I think we should start at the bar where they met. You OK going into a bar?" I said. Knowing Buck was a reformed alcoholic, I had to ask.

"No, problem. They serve diet Sprite, don't they?" he said.

Bob Moats

I took David Weston's picture out of the file Benson gave me, and we headed out. Buck wanted to drive so I let him. We headed up to Mt. Clemens, driving up the same roads we traveled during the Classmate Murders. It was déjà vu.

In Mt. Clemens, we drove down Walnut Street and parked on a side street. We walked around till we found the Midnight Bar and went in. It was dark, smelled of beer and urine, not a high class place. Buck and I sauntered over to the bar, and I signaled to the semi-attractive barmaid. She slowly walked over and leaned on the counter, flashing a pair of breasts in a tank top that barely held them back. Her tank top said "Available for Nursing." I resisted.

"And what will you two cuties have?" she asked in a cigarette abused voice.

"I'm Jim, this is Buck, and you are?"

"Call me Dolly, but I answer to just about anything." She smiled.

I ordered a Pepsi, and Buck grunted out diet Sprite. She stared at us, and asked if we were cops.

"No, I'm private, my friend here is my enforcer," I said, smiling.

She looked at Buck. He was standing tall, all six foot three of him, and he grinned at her. She went to get our drinks. I watched her to be sure she opened the cans in front of me. She did. She brought them back, and I said I didn't want a glass.

"I clean my glasses regular," she said defensively.

"I've never liked messing up a glass when I can drink from the can, no offense."

"So, you two aren't here for the ambiance of this joint, and the cops have already asked every question I could answer. So what do you want?"

"Did they show you a picture of David Weston?" I said as I flipped it to her.

"Yep, they did, although this one is different."

"How so?" I asked.

"It doesn't look like the other pictures I was shown. Where'd you get this one?" she asked.

"From his lawyer. Is this very different from the ones the cops showed you?"

"Yeah, it's a different face, close, but I'm good at faces, and this one is different."

"So have you seen the face in this picture?"

"Yeah, I've seen him in here a number of times. He's a stalker. Watches for lonely women, then hits on them and they all follow him out of the bar.

I looked at Buck. "Why would the cops show a different photo of this guy? They covering up something, or got the wrong guy?"

I would have to call the lawyer about this. "The picture the cops showed you, you couldn't identify the man?"

"I told them I hadn't seen the face they showed me," she said. "I don't follow the news so I didn't see the guy, other than what they asked me."

I was confused. "The night of the murders, do you remember this guy in here?" Pointing to my picture.

"I worked that night. Yeah, he was in here."

"Did he leave with anyone?" I asked.

"I remember a quiet brunette that he talked up. I didn't see them leave together though. After a while, he and she were gone, but I didn't see them leave together."

"Could you identify her or do you know her?"

Dominatrix Murders

"She comes in maybe once a week. She says she's trying to get away from her family so she comes here to have a few bracers then goes back home."

"When was the last time she was here?"

"When I saw her with the guy in that photo, last week. Hasn't been back since."

I took out my business card and said, "If she comes in, please call me right away." I handed her the card and a twenty dollar bill. She smiled at both.

"You got it, P.I., I'll call right away." She went off to take care of some guy yelling for a beer.

I looked at Buck, "Something's wrong with this picture, the big picture, not the little pictures. You know what I mean."

He laughed. "Yeah, I do. The cops either got the wrong picture or someone is trying to frame Weston," he said.

"Yep, my thoughts exactly." I pulled out my cell phone and called Benson, I got his voice mail, and I hated that. I left a message for him to call me, that it was important.

"Buck, are you interested in a swimming pool for your backyard?" I asked.

He looked at me with a puzzled expression, "Why, do I need one?"

"No, but that's what Ralph Flagg sells, pools and spas. May as well go fit him in while we wait on the mystery woman."

We downed our drinks, I waved at the barmaid and we left. It was good to be back out in fresh air. The bar had that smell like Mt. Clemens used to have all over, a stink from the mineral baths that were a rage back in the '20s to the '50s. The whole town had a sulfur, rotten egg smell to it. The years had taken away the baths and the smell. Now the air was fresh again.

We drove down Groesbeck Highway to the Lazy Daze Pools and Spas, parked and went in.

From his picture, I recognized the man who set his sights on us and strode over quickly was Ralph. "Afternoon, gentlemen. Interested in a pool or maybe a spa to rest your weary bones?" He rattled on about this pool or that spa and herded us around the store before we could even say anything.

I hated hard sell salespeople, and I didn't like Ralph from minute one. I really couldn't see what Elma saw in him, other than a glib tongue.

"Excuse me, take a breath. I am looking for a spa that can handle about 15 to 20 people," I said.

His eyes glowed. "Now why would you need a spa that large?"

"I have friends that are into having a good time, if you know what I mean. We have sort of a club, and we get a little loose with each other, and I thought a spa would be a nice ice breaker."

"Hmm, is this a swingers club, may I ask?" He was drooling.

"I hate to put names on things, but it's something like that. We get into keys, swinging and kink." I spread it on.

I almost could see his eyes roll back into his head. He paused for a bit then said, "Is it a private club, or can anyone come?"

"Well." I moved my head to his nametag. "May I call you Ralph?" He said I could. "I'd have to get approval from our group, but if you were interested, I could see. Are you a member of any other clubs that I may mention to give you a rep?"

He smiled. "I'm a member of the Dark Dungeon B and D Club in Pontiac. Is that something that would qualify me?" He was anxious now.

"That may help. We don't do very much bondage, but we like swapping. You into that?"

"I enjoy it, but my wife is not into it at all. Would that be a problem?"

"Well, we have members who are in the same position, more women than men, but it's not a problem. Give me your card and I'll see what I can do to get you an interview. There is a membership fee, too, a grand to join. It helps fund our parties."

He was salivating now and handed me his card. "I have money, no problem."

"OK, I'll be in touch soon." I looked to Buck, and we went out.

Buck smiled and said, the boy is hot to trot.

*

Chapter Five

My thoughts were on Ralph and what a sleaze ball he was. I wondered why he was working at the pool place if he was living off Elma. I'd have to ask her about it. My other mystery was why did the police show a different photo of Weston? Did someone screw up, or was there a cover up for some reason? Did they not want the barmaid to ID him so they could say he lied about being with the woman? I was hoping for the photo screw up, and not some conspiracy to cover the murder of his wife. Why would they want to cover it up? Did they have an idea who actually committed the murder and were protecting someone? I was hoping Benson could sort the mess out.

We were heading back to my office when my cell phone rang. It was Benson. "Hello," I said.

"Jim, got your message. I was in court. What's up?"

"I have a mystery. That picture of Weston that you gave me, I showed it to the barmaid at the bar where he supposedly picked up the mystery woman, and she said that was not the same picture the police showed her, not the same guy."

He was silent for a minute. "You're saying the police showed her a photo of someone who was not Weston?"

"I think that's what I said, yes. She said they had a picture of someone else, and she said the guy in their photo wasn't in the bar that night. The picture you gave me, she said he was there, and with a woman. What's going on?" I asked.

"Good question. I'll have to call the DA and find out where they got their picture. You really sure about the barmaid?"

"She didn't seem like she was trying to screw the pooch. I took her at her word."

"OK, I'll do some checking here and get back to you. Are you going to follow up on your findings?"

"Yeah, I'm going to try and track down the woman who was seen with Weston that night at the bar. I'll let you know what I find."

"Thanks for the heads up. I'll check on it." he said good bye and hung up.

We were just pulling back into my parking lot. I looked at Buck and said, "The plot thickens."

We went in, and I saw Elma Flagg sitting in the lobby. "Elma, is there anything wrong?"

"I'm sorry, I was just hoping you had something for me," she said quietly.

"Well, you were just here yesterday. I have done some investigating, and I could fill you in, but I really think I need to gather a bit more info before I give you my findings. Just to be accurate. Can you wait a day or two more?"

She looked sad and said she would. I introduced Buck as my assistant, and Buck did his charming way of greeting her. She smiled wide at Buck, giggled, and said she'd let us go to do our thing. I said I did have some info, but I'd let her know at least by the day after tomorrow. She thanked me and left. I felt bad for her, considering the rat she was married to. I entered my office followed by Buck and checked my answering machine. No messages.

"That skunk Ralph should be hung out to dry for hurting that sweet woman," Buck growled.

I guess Buck saw more to Elma than I did. That made me feel a bit bad that I might have misjudged her. She was not the most beautiful woman, but that sad creature I saw in the hall just melted my heart.

"I'm going to see to it that Ralphy boy goes down hard," I swore. "Son of a bitch."

It was now about 3 p.m., and we had accomplished a little bit of good. I was happy to know Ralph was a creep, and tomorrow I would bring his world to a speedy halt. I had recorded our conversation at the pool place with my new Palm Treo cell phone, for proof to play for Elma.

I looked up to the wall and admired my last Palm Treo that saved my life from a bullet in the desert of Vegas. I attached it and the bullet that nearly took my life inside a nice small display case I bought at a craft store and got a little engraved plate to say why it was on the wall. As soon as I got back to Michigan, I bought another Treo, and hoped it would protect me like its predecessor.

I told Buck to go home and we could start early in the morning, but not before 9 a.m. I closed up shop after he exited and got to my car just as my cell phone rang. The caller ID said it was Benson. I answered.

"That was quick. Find out anything on the photo?" I asked.

"Not yet, but I got you the interview with Weston at the Macomb County jail. Just go in and mention my name to whoever is at the sign in booth. They'll take it from there."

"Thanks, I'll head up there now. If you could find out about the photos, I don't want to be caught uninformed when I snoop."

"I'm making it a priority. I called the DA's office and I got someone inside checking on it. I'll let you know as soon as I hear."

I said thanks and hung up. I drove up Groesbeck Highway to Elizabeth Road where the county jail, courthouse and Sheriff's offices were. I parked and went into the jail waiting room. There were a good number of people sitting around waiting for incarcerated loved ones to get out or to post bail. They all had that same tired, miserable look on their faces, like they had it with junior's little crime sprees and were wondering why they should put their houses up in lieu of bail.

Dominatrix Murders

I went to the two inch Plexiglas protected booth. Talking into the round metal plate that housed the microphone, I told the woman deputy my name and my purpose. She looked at a clipboard of paper and pointed to a door on my left. I went in, got to another Plexiglas booth, and explained again my purpose. A big deputy came out and had me place all my personal property, including my gun, on a tray. He placed the tray in a wire cage and gave me a ticket to retrieve my stuff. They let me keep the file folder I carried after looking through it for, I presumed, weapons or explosives.

He told me to follow him through three sliding doors, each having to be buzzed open. We got to a row of small rooms, one of which he told me to wait inside. After about fifteen minutes of waiting, the door opened again, and another deputy brought in Weston. At least this guy looked like the picture I had.

He sat across from me, still handcuffed, and the deputy shackled him to his chair. The deputy said he'd be right outside if I needed help. I looked at Weston and introduced myself.

"May I call you Dave?" I asked.

"Yeah, whatever," he said quietly.

"I've been hired by Mark Benson to find the woman you were with the night your wife was murdered. Are you going to help me?"

"I didn't kill my wife. I told them that, and they say I lied about that night. Yeah, I'm going to help you."

"OK, starting from the beginning, you were in the Midnight Bar in Mt. Clemens and met with the woman in question. What was her name?"

"She said her name was Cindy. She didn't want to talk about herself too much since she was married and wasn't in the bar to be picked up. I chatted her up a while, and she started getting looser. The drinks helped. She said her husband was always out of town, and she was tired of sitting around waiting for him."

"She didn't tell you where she lived, city or anything that might help?"

"Nope, she was very secretive about it."

"OK, Dave, now give me your take on why your wife was murdered."

He sat quietly for a while. I was getting impatient. "Help me out here, Dave. You could be put away for a very long time."

Dominatrix Murders

He leaned forward, said quietly, "You're here to help me, right? Everything I tell you is privileged, right?"

"Just like your lawyer," I said.

He paused again, and then said, "My wife had a little business on the side, something our family never knew, or our children. Noreen, that's her name, had a little office where she would do therapy for people. People who had issues with authority."

"What kind of authority issues, Dave?"

"Do you know anything about dominance?" he asked even quieter. I had to lean in more to hear him. He continued, "Noreen would help people who wanted to be submissive to another person, usually because they were in a position of authority over other people, and it ate at them. So Noreen would be their dominant figure, making them feel less than what they were."

I was stunned, three times in a week this subject came up. "Noreen was a Dominatrix?" I asked.

"Yeah, they call it that, but she didn't like the name. She referred to herself as an 'attitude adjuster.' She wasn't in it for the bondage stuff or sex. There was absolutely no sex with her clients. But the stuff she did was still bondage no matter what you call it. They came, took it in, and left happy. And she was paid well for it."

"Did you tell the police about this?"

"Hell, no. They would have spread it to the media and it would have destroyed our families."

"Well, all destruction aside, this might have given the police something more to go on for her murder. It might have cleared you."

"I don't think so. Noreen never really talked much about her business, but she did say she had some very powerful people as clients. They could be behind it, and I'm the scapegoat. I don't think I'm going to beat this."

"You will if I can do anything about it. Where was Noreen's office, and can I get in?"

"It's in a little strip mall, on Gratiot Avenue by Utica Road. At the end of the building. There's a small sign on the door saying 'Noreen Black, Attitude Therapist.' Black is a name she made up. You can talk to Willy in the novelty shop. He's the building manager, he'll get you in. Just say I sent you. He knows me."

I told him I would be back and I would do everything I could to clear him, hopefully without damaging Noreen's reputation. I signaled to the guard, he came in, and unshackled Weston, then they went out. Another guard took me out to the room where I got my property back. The deputy asked if I was trying to clear Weston, I said that's what I was hired for. He just stared at me as if I was a bug and said nothing. I thanked him and went out.

Why did I feel like things were going to get complicated?

*

Chapter Six

It was just after 5 p.m., and I was getting run down. I headed to the house and Penny. I got there, and her car was in the drive. She must have been out after her show since she usually put it in the garage. She opened the door as I came up and latched on to me giving me a good tonsil search.

"What did I do to deserve that, and why aren't you in sexy lingerie for a greeting like that?" I kidded.

"I just missed you, and glad you didn't get shot today," she said with a smile.

"You had some kind of sex talk on your show today, and now you're horny?" I hoped.

"No, we discussed family trees, and how to trace your ancestors. It was a good show."

We both went to the couch and sat. I laid my head back and related my day to her. She sat nodding her head as I talked. She started looking like a bobble head. I said I wanted to watch her show, so she went to turn on the TiVo and we watched. I made my usual comments about the show that I made every day, she listened and we discussed ways to keep her show interesting.

She bounced up and said she had lasagna in the oven and it was about ready. We ate on the couch and watched TV for a while. Around 6:30 p.m., my cell rang and the caller ID said 'private.' I didn't like those calls. They were usually some sales persons, but I answered, ready to yell at someone. It was Benson.

"What's up? Any good news?" I asked.

"The Roseville cops say there was a mix up with the pictures. The primary detective on the case got the file from another cop who started the case but was pulled off at the last minute. He hadn't met with Weston, just had the picture, so he used that. That's what they're saying, but I'm doubtful. They did a lot of tap dancing around the thing. Something's up. The primary detective's name is

Dominatrix Murders

Ben Lincoln," he said, all in one breath. I could see why he was a lawyer.

"Well, I got some revelations to tell you, too. There may be something more to this case than we think." I told him of my discussion with Weston and that I was going to search the office in the morning. He took in everything I said, and I could tell his wheels were turning.

"People in high places maybe murder to cover up impropriety by some official person who felt threatened that he'd be revealed as a submissive," he said.

"You trying to take my job now?" I laughed. "I deduced that, too. Tomorrow I hope to dig up some info at her office. I'll let you know what I find."

He said thanks and hung up. I looked at Penny and asked if she wanted to take a ride to play detective. She said it made her all goose bumps and agreed. We went out to my car and drove over to Gratiot Avenue and down to Utica Road. I scanned the corner for the right strip mall and spotted a novelty shop, figuring that was the one. Guess that's why I'm a detective. I parked out front, and Penny and I went into the small store. It was filled with all kinds of gags, novelties and a few magic props. I was looking over their selection of tricks when a rather smallish man came up and asked if he could help me.

"I'm looking for Willy," I said.

He smiled and said, "You got him, what can I do for you?"

"Dave Weston said you could help me get into his wife's office." I showed him my I.D. and he looked closely at it.

"Wow, a real private eye. First one I've ever met. Sure, I can let you in. Too bad about Noreen and Dave. They were such a nice couple. I wasn't sure what to do about the office, but Noreen paid three months in advance like clockwork, so it's still there till I hear from Dave. Hold on while I get the key." He skittered off and I noticed Penny was looking at some toys in the adult section. I said not to get any ideas.

She pointed to a blow up doll, and said, "I'd agree to a three-way with that."

I laughed, remembering our adventures at the strip bar in Vegas and the hot dancer who hit on Penny. Willy came back and led us out of the building and down to the far end on the side of the building where there was a small office.

Willy got up to the door and stopped. "What the hell, the door's been jimmied." He pushed it open and we went in. The place was definitely ransacked. Noreen's files and papers were all over the floor, and the desk was pulled apart. I went into the next room. It was small with chains and ropes hanging from the walls. A table with straps on the sides, I presumed used to bind someone down, was overturned. Other bondage paraphernalia, some I recognized from Penny's show the other day, were hanging or lying on the floor.

"Looks like someone was trying to find something," I said.

Willy just said, "Wow, I've never been in this room since Noreen moved in. This is very interesting." He was picking up bondage toys and had a strange smile on his face.

I said to Penny, "This break-in has got to have something to do with the murder of Noreen. Someone knew her and her work and needed to get something out of here."

She agreed.

I told Willy we'd be in here for a little while and I would see that the door was secured. He said he had to get back to his store and to let him know if we needed anything. He went out.

I asked Penny if she would go get my Fuji digital camera out of the car. I was just looking around, taking in the whole place, trying not to disturb anything till Penny came back. She brought me the camera, and I shot a good number of pictures of the rooms then said we needed to see if we could find anything incriminating. I didn't think we would, the place was already hit pretty good. We dug through the few papers that were there, but found nothing special, just info on "treatments" as she called them. No names to be found, just numbers to denote her clients. I was sure she didn't have that good of a memory, so there must be a book or file with names and numbers to go by.

I was going around knocking on the walls, hoping to find a secret panel. Nothing gave. I took a chair with straps out of the back room and stood on it to see over the tall walled box that housed the furnace. Nothing on top. I up righted the desk and stood on it, pushing a ceiling tile over and looking around above the ceiling. I couldn't see anything up there, either. The drawers on the desk were all pulled out so I figured the person checked inside the desk. We came up with nothing after an exhaustive search, and it was starting to get late, so I said to pack it in. We went out, and I made sure the door was secure. I stopped to let Willy know we were leaving, and I told him I would check with Dave about the office. He thanked me and we left.

We got back, Penny pulled her car in the garage, and I parked on the side like I usually do. We went in, and Penny said she felt grubby from the sex shop and was going to take a nice long bath. She asked if I wanted to join her. I said I was going to make a few phone calls and we could pick up in the bedroom. She zipped off to the bathroom, and I got on my phone and called Buck. He was his usual chipper self, and I told him all that happened after he left. He said he was just going to have to move in with us so he wouldn't miss all the fun. I told Buck I was going to call Benson, and then I would see him in the morning at the office. He agreed and hung up.

I called Benson's cell phone number and got his voice mail. I left a message and put the phone down. I sat back organizing all my thoughts of the day. It was a busy one. Got a few things started and would nail Ralph tomorrow. I would have more info and a possible divorce lawyer for Elma. I smiled. There was not much else I could do right then, so I thought about that offer to share a bath with my favorite girl. Crime could wait one more day. I took her offer.

*

Chapter Seven

We were up early and getting ready to go to our respective jobs. Penny said she had a couple of home improvement guys on her show today. I hoped she didn't start remodeling the house now. We kissed, and she went off. I always worried about her and that long drive to her studio on the freeways. She was a big girl, and I knew she was careful, but there are way too many idiots on the roads for me not to worry. I had to take it in stride.

I got to my office around 8:50, and Buck was there in his usual resting position in the lobby. I kicked his feet this time, and he jumped up, but I had already backed off, anticipating his automatic response.

"Good morning, Jimmy. How are you this fine morning?" He gave me his big walrus smile that always brightened my day.

"Well, I'm hoping we can do some good for the world and make it a better place to live in," I said.

He laughed. "At least make Elma's life better."

"Yep, and I'm hoping I don't have any more B&D people popping up." I opened the door to my office, and we went in. I sat at my desk, bringing up a camera case just as my cell phone rang. It was Benson.

"Good morning," I said. "I've got some more interesting details for you." I told him about the office mess and what my feelings on the case were, and he agreed. Something more was going on. I just needed to find the mystery woman. I said I'd like to talk to the primary detective on Weston's case.

Dominatrix Murders

Benson said to be careful if there were cops involved. I said I'd watch my hide, and we finished.

I dialed Trapper's number, and he came on. I asked if he had a minute to spare. He said crime had stopped for the day just for me, so he had time to talk. I spent the next twenty minutes filling him in on what we came up with on Ralph then gave him all the gory details on the Weston case. I explained about my checking with the barmaid and showing her my photo and about the police showing a different photo. He said that sounded queer to him, something was off.

"To mix up ID photos comes under three headings, carelessness, stupidity or a cover-up," Trapper offered. "It sounds like a cover-up to me."

I agreed.

"Do you know this Detective Lincoln on the Roseville squad?" I asked.

"I've heard a little about him, ambitious, arrogant, asshole, the three A's of evil." He laughed. "But I wouldn't trust him from what I hear."

"Could he have been a customer of Noreen's and took over the case to cover himself?" I asked.

"Anything's possible. If he was involved in the murder, it would be easy for him to bury the evidence since no one else is going to nose around in his case. Let me snoop around my precinct, see if anyone knows more about him. I'll call you if I find anything," he offered.

"Buck's here with me. Want to say anything to him?" I asked.

He said he had nothing to say to Buck.

Buck yelled, "Catch any good hookers lately, Trapper?"

I heard Trapper growl and say, "You just had to tell him what Weber said, didn't you?"

"Just trying to be fair with everyone, keeping all concerned on the same footing," I said.

"Thanks, Richards, I love you, too." He hung up. I was going to have to ask him about his aversion to saying good-bye.

"Buck, are you good at handling a video camera? I don't mean for porn, either."

Buck smiled and said he knew which end was which. I opened the camera case and handed him my Sony Handicam and showed him the functions of the buttons. I said I had a wireless microphone under my shirt and I attached a receiver to the camcorder, turned them both on and spoke into the mic. Buck was listening through the headphones from the receiver, and said it came through loud and clear. I told him to keep listening and went out the door, down the hall, still talking. I was outside the building then came back in. Buck said it never lost contact.

I packed the camcorder in the case and said, "Time to capture a pervert." We headed out.

I parked my car in front of the pool store facing the windows. I set the thing up for Buck and told him my plan. He loved it. I went in the building and got some twerpy looking guy in a pastel green shirt. I asked for Ralph, and he said he could help me. I asked again for Ralph. He grumbled and went off to the back room. I waved at Buck in the car videotaping me and asked if he could hear me. He waved. Good, I thought, now to get Ralphy on tape.

"Hey, I remember you." He smiled as he came from the back room. "Any word on my acceptance to your club?" I took his arm and led him to the window, looking back at the display room, saying it was more private up here. He agreed as if we had some secret talk to do.

I carefully looked out to Buck who waved again, and then back to Ralph. "OK, I have just a bit more interviewing to do with you for the review board."

He said shoot, he had nothing to hide.

I took out a slip of paper I wrote on while I was awake in bed that morning and read, "First, are you seriously interested in joining our swingers group?"

He said yes, enthusiastically.

"OK, your wife isn't interested in swinging?"

"My wife is a prude. We have sex a lot only because I enjoy it. I could put a bag over her head and be just as happy." That's it, Ralph, hang yourself.

"Explain your membership in the Dark Dungeon B&D club."

"I met this chick in a bar one night, and we got to talking about sex. She said she was into kinky things. She told me about this club in Pontiac and said she could get me in if I was interested. We drove out there, and it was fantastic. Best sex I have had in years." He grinned.

"I thought they weren't into sex in bondage clubs?" I asked.

"Well, once you're in a room, anything goes, but they check on you first, make sure you aren't a cop."

I thought Trapper's friend on Pontiac PD might like to hear that.

I continued, "OK, I said there is a membership fee. You have enough money to fund your pleasures?"

"Hey, my wife is rich. I got funds coming out the ass." He smiled.

"If your wife is rich, why are you working here?" I had to ask that question.

"My wife says I have to contribute to the marriage, otherwise I get nothing from her. I show I'm working at this stinking job, and she gives me my toys. This job is no killer, and I get to be away from her." Well, that answered that.

"Have you ever been married before this?"

"I was married twice, tragic marriages, both wives are dead."

"Were either of those wives into swapping or kink?" I asked.

"Hell, no, they were just as frigid as my present wife."

"Ralph, what is your goal if accepted as a member of our group?"

"To have great sex with as many women as I can. Isn't that the goal of every man?"

I wanted to punch his lights out, but said, "Oh, yes, we all have that goal, don't we?"

"So you're having regular sex at the bondage club. Doesn't your wife wonder why her sex is cut back?" I asked.

"I give it to her when she's getting in a bitchy mood about it, doing my duty for the cause." He smirked.

"Do you plan on staying with your wife if you get into our club?"

"Hell, yes, as long as the money is there, I'll stay and slip it to her once in a while, keep her happy." He grinned.

I really wanted to punch this guy. "OK, I have enough to take back to the board. I'll get back to you shortly."

He shook my hand, and I left. Once in the car, I said to Buck, "You got it all?"

"I'm a regular **Steven Spielberg**. Elma's going to love our movie." He grinned.

We went back to the office, and I took the tape out of the Handicam and put it in my fire-proof lock box.

It was almost 11:30 a.m., and I was wondering what to do next about Weston's case.

I looked at Buck and said, "I'll call Elma in a while and have her come in tomorrow." Buck said he wanted to be there. I said he'd have front row seats and popcorn.

Chapter Eight

Buck said if I didn't need him, he had some running to do. I said to go enjoy himself and call before he came back to be sure I was in. He left, and I began reading the file on Weston that Benson gave me. I wondered if it was a copy of the police file or just the lawyer's copy. As I was staring off into space, my cell phone rang. It was Trapper.

"Hello, super cop," I said.

"Don't try and butter me up. I'm still mad at you for telling Buck about my troubled youth." I could tell he was smiling. "I did a bit of detective work. I do that, you know. It's my job, and I even get paid for it. I talked to some people here who used to work in Roseville. Not a one of them had a good word to say about Lincoln. He has a rep for being a cowboy, doesn't follow the rules all the time. If he can bend them, he will. One guy here said he thought Lincoln was into some shady activities, even hints of B&D. Sound familiar?" I could tell Trapper was eating it up.

"Well, he could be the link then, but I can't go in and accuse a police detective of murder and conspiracy," I said.

"Not if you want to stay alive, knowing he may be behind it," Trapper warned.

"I guess I'll have to try and prove Weston's innocence and let the police figure out who did it."

"That's a plan. I'll back you with anything you need that's in my jurisdiction. Just keep me informed," he said.

I thought he was about to hang up and told him to hold on. "I have a question that I have wanted to ask you ever since the classmate murders. Every time you're done with talking on the phone or leaving a room, you don't say good-bye. It's just a courtesy thing, but you don't do it. Why?"

He was quiet for a bit. I gave him the leeway. He hemmed a while then said, "I'll tell you, but it goes no further than this. You tell Buck, and I'll hunt you down and waste you. Understood?" I said I agreed. "I'm telling you this because it's something very personal and sometimes it's good to share with someone. I was young when my father died. I told you before that I was in police academy when it happened, and he was a cop, too. I lived with my parents when they moved to North Las Vegas while I was in academy. One day my dad and I had an argument, and I stormed out of the house saying good-bye rather harshly. Later that day he was killed on duty in a gang related shoot out. I regretted the way I said good-bye to him. It took me a long time to get over it. Then two years later, I was living with a wonderful woman, and one day we had a fight and I said I was leaving and stormed out, again yelling good-bye to her. She was killed in a head on collision that afternoon. That was the day I stopped saying good-bye. I didn't want to lose another person I cared about." He went silent and hung up.

I was a bit stunned and reached for a tissue. I didn't know what to do now. I thought about going up to the Midnight Bar and asking around about the mystery woman. I reached for the phone and dialed Elma. She came on, and I asked her if she could come in tomorrow morning. She asked if I had any good news. I said I would cover everything then. She was quiet and then said she'd be in. Now I felt even worse, hearing my friend tell me his story and having to burst a poor woman's bubble about her cheating husband. I took refuge in the fact that I was exposing a cheat, and hopefully she would deal with it. I would recommend Benson as a divorce lawyer, if it came to that. But I still felt bad.

Bob Moats

Around 3 p.m., I was fidgeting with some files on my desk when the door opened and a gorgeous redhead stepped in and asked where the travel agency was. I told her, she thanked me and left. I thought about opening up my own travel agency. I sure as hell wasn't getting the good looking ones.

My cell phone rang and I looked. Just the phone number, didn't know who it could be, so I answered it.

"Mr. P.I., this is Dolly from the Midnight Bar. You told me to call if that woman showed up. Well, she's here," she said excitedly.

I told her I was about 15 minutes away, and asked if she could stall her, talk to her, buy her drinks on me, anything to keep her there. I was on my way. I hung up and did my best to keep within the speed limit but was pushing it. I got to the bar and entered.

Dolly saw me and motioned to a woman sitting at the back end of the bar by the wall. I went over and sat next to her, looked at her and nodded my head.

"Go away, I'm not interested," she said, glancing at me.

"Yeah, well, neither am I," I said. "But there are other people interested in you. It would be in your best of health to talk to me."

Dominatrix Murders

She was silent then started to get up. I grabbed her arm and sat her back down.

"Hey, that hurts, I'll call the cops!" she wailed.

"Go ahead. I'd like that, so you can explain to them why you went to a motel with David Weston on the night his wife was butchered. Go ahead and call the cops, or do you want me to do it for you?" I threatened.

She was deadly silent for a full minute, just staring at the bar top, and then spoke softly. "I had nothing to do with any murders."

"I didn't say you did. I just want to know if you were with Weston that night."

"What did you mean it would be in my best health to talk?" she asked.

"I think there is something going on. The police are possibly not interested in clearing Weston, and you could be someone they don't want talking. Get what I mean? So far you don't exist, but that could change. I can get you protection with Weston's lawyer if you want to stay alive." I knew I was spreading it on thick, but I had to convince this woman to come in and testify, so I lied a bit.

"I have a family, I don't want to get involved," she said.

64

"I understand. Just talk to the lawyer, and we can work things out for you. That's all it takes." I hoped I wouldn't have to resort to unpleasant actions.

She looked at me and said, "I read what happened to that woman. I'm sorry it happened. Yes, I was with Dave when she was killed. I was afraid to say anything. I didn't want my husband or children to know I was having a fling. But I felt guilty about Dave being blamed. I came here to see if I was remembered. I guess I was."

"I'll be sure you're protected, my pledge, even though you don't know me. I'll deal with it. I'm also a licensed private investigator. I carry a big gun."

I asked the woman her name. She said Marylou. I told her my name and said that Dave called her by another name. She said she lied and told him Cindy. I knew I had the right woman.

She smiled and asked what she should do. I said to follow me out of the bar quietly and then I would take her some place safe to talk to the lawyer. She agreed. I got out my cell phone and called Benson. He came on.

"I've got the woman. She needs protection. Where can we meet?"

Dominatrix Murders

"Bring her to my office, and we'll decide what to do." I said I'd be there in about twenty minutes and hung up.

I took her hand and got her on her feet. I waved to the barmaid and put another twenty on the bar. She came over and said I'd be welcome anytime. Marylou and I left the building and headed to my car. We were just about ready to turn the corner of the building to the parking lot on the side when I felt something zing past my ear, immediately followed by the sound of a shot as a bullet struck the building. I pushed Marylou to the ground and covered her the best I could while I drew my Glock out and pointed it in the direction I thought the shot came from. One more shot came and hit the pavement as I fired a couple rounds towards a car on the street. It sped off, but not before I blew out its rear window. I looked at Marylou and said, "Well, I warned you."

*

Chapter Nine

I quickly got Marylou to my car and pulled out my cell phone. I speed dialed Trapper. He came on, and I explained what was going on and what just happened. I said I was about five minutes from Clinton Township precinct and twenty minutes from Benson, and I wanted police protection right now. He said to get my ass in quickly and be careful. I drove out of the lot and headed down Groesbeck to the police headquarters where trapper and Officer Becker were waiting out front. I hadn't seen Becker since the classmate murders, and he greeted me.

"Guys, this is Marylou Martin. She admits to being with Dave Weston during the time his wife was murdered."

They said their hellos, and Trapper said to me, "I called Benson and told him we were bringing her in, but I didn't think it's a good idea for her to be anywhere near Roseville right now. He agreed. Mark really has no place for her to be safe now that someone knows she exists.

"What am I supposed to do? I don't want to die!" Marylou wailed. I put my hand on her shoulder and told her to calm down, we weren't going to let anything happen to her. I looked at Trapper. He shrugged.

"She's a material witness to a crime and her life is definitely in danger. She needs protection," I demanded.

"Yes, we can hold her here over night till the DA and Prosecutor's offices talk to her. We'll take her in and get her statement on record, but it's not our jurisdiction. Roseville may want to take her in there," Trapper offered.

"Oh, yea, let them get careless with their handling of the witness. Maybe she'll fall down a flight of stairs," I argued.

"Jim, I understand, but there is a process we have to abide by. It's the law. We have nothing to hold her for."

I knew Trapper didn't like the system. I had an idea. I took Marylou's arm and swung her hand to Trapper's face and nearly knocked him over. I misjudged my aim. He came back and said "What the hell are you doing?"

I yelled, "Arrest this woman, she just assaulted an officer of the law!"

Trapper looked at me and smiled. He turned to Becker and said to escort Mrs. Martin into lock up. He told her she can't be assaulting police and she would have to suffer the consequences. She was wide eyed and not sure what the hell we were up to, but she knew she was going to be away from anyone wanting to kill her. Trapper looked at me and said "You could have warned me."

I said, "What fun would that be?" He grinned.

We sat in Trapper's office. I asked how they knew to follow me to the Midnight Bar. I only talked on my cell phone. They couldn't have bugged that.

"You went to Noreen's office. They may have been watching that," Trapper offered. "Cops are good at tailing people. They could have been watching you for days once they knew you were on the case. Bringing a woman out of that bar sent up flags."

"Geez, I let myself be watched. Says a lot for my P.I. skills," I lamented.

Trapper laughed. "You've been a P.I. for all of four months. You can't expect to have the experience in that short of time. You learn as you go."

"Well, from now on I'm going to be suspicious of everyone and everything," I said.

Mark Benson popped his head in the door. "Any good cops still around this place?" he joked. He came in and sat. "I brought a steno to take Martin's statements. I am so glad she was found." He looked at me. "Thanks." Then at Trapper. "She's locked up for assaulting a cop? Good ploy. It will keep her away from the beast of Roseville until we get everything in writing. We can suppress her identity, make her a key witness under protection until we get Weston released. Then the cops will have to investigate to find the real murderer. I talked to Weston and convinced him to give his statements about his wife's activities that may have involved officials." He looked at me. "You'll have to make a statement as to how you found her and what transpired after you did. Glad neither of you were killed."

"Thanks, I'm glad I wasn't killed, too," I said. "I'll write up a statement and sign it here tomorrow with Trapper as witness. Right now I have another case I'm not looking forward to, but it has to be done." I looked at Benson. "I may have a woman who will need a divorce lawyer or criminal lawyer if she murders her husband."

Benson laughed and said, "Those cases are the hardest, telling a woman her husband is a louse. I don't envy you. I'll give her my best at taking him for everything," he said.

I said good-bye to everyone and headed out. I called Buck and asked what he was up to. He said, not much. I said to meet me at the office, we had some surveillance to do. He said he'd be there. I was in a strange mood. I had been shot at today and I saved a man from prison, but I had mixed feelings. I needed to put up a tiny shell around my feelings to get through playing detective, not take cases so hard.

I drove back to my office and gathered my camera equipment as Buck strolled in. He asked what we were up to, and I said I wanted more proof of Ralph's indiscretions, just to be iron clad in our accusations as to his screwing around. I sat at my desk, called the pool place, and asked for Ralph. He came on. I reminded him who I was, and said the committee was considering his request to join, but needed some proof he was a member of the B&D club in Pontiac. I apologized but said they have to be careful to qualify our members. He said, no problem, he could go get a receipt from the club tonight since he was going there anyway, and would have it for me in the morning. I said that would work.

I looked to Buck and said we needed to take a trip out to Pontiac. I packed the camera gear, and we went out to the car. I stopped and said I had to call Penny to explain why I wasn't going to be home right away. He laughed and said something about being pussy whipped. I said it was too bad he didn't have a pussy whipper. He looked at me funny like and then laughed out loud.

Dominatrix Murders

I went off to the side of the parking lot and called Penny. She answered saying "Perverts are Us. How may I screw you?"

"I certainly hope you looked at caller I.D. or I'll be a little pissed," I said.

"Oh, sweetie, you are my only pervert. What do you want? I'm in the middle of having great sex with Eric."

"Are you going to start that again?" I demanded. "I just called to say Buck and I are going to a B&D club tonight, and I'll be a little late."

I could hear her breathing, then she said, "And I don't get to go? You can take me to a strip club in Vegas but not a bondage club here? That is so wrong."

"I'll make it up to you. We'll go to a strip club this weekend, and we'll even take our big son with us."

"I'm sure Buck will love that." She laughed. "So, what's up for tonight?"

"I'm on Elma Flagg's case, and Buck and I are going to get some pictures of hubby in action. I'm going to fry him good so Elma can take him for everything."

Bob Moats

"Wow, you're mean. I like that. I just may give up Eric for you." I could tell she was smiling wide. She said to be careful and hung up.

Sometimes she drove me crazy, but I didn't know what I would do without her. I went back to Buck. He was making little whipping noises. I looked at him and said to stop it or Penny and I wouldn't take him to a strip club that weekend. His mouth opened, but nothing came out. I said to get in the car, and we drove out.

We got to Pontiac just before 6 p.m. I said Ralph would probably head over there after he closed up the pool store at 5:30, so we could wait here for him. I had checked my Palm TX map program for the address of the B&D club, and we were across the street from it. We sat waiting. After about ten minutes a Pontiac police cruiser pulled up next to us and rolled down his window asking what our business was.

I got out of the car, came around, showed him my I.D., and explained we were waiting for a stray husband to show up to get him on camera. I also told him about our finding out the club does front for sex. He said they were watching the club, too, which was why they kept an eye out for strangers in the area. I told him about Trapper and his connection with someone in the Pontiac police and what I knew from my case. He thanked me and said to be extra careful, the club had some powerful connections. I said I was just after a little fish and wouldn't rattle any cages. I gave him my business card, and they drove off.

I got back in the car, looked at Buck and said this could be an interesting night.

*

Chapter Ten

About fifteen minutes later Ralph drove up and parked in a no parking zone, dumb shit. I took out my HP M22 pocket camera and put it in my shirt pocket. I said to Buck, let's roll. We got out of the car and went across the street as Ralph was walking up to the entrance.

"Ralph! Hold up," I yelled, he turned with a stunned look not expecting someone to call his name in this neighborhood. He saw Buck and me, and got a smile on his face.

"What are you two doing here?" he asked.

"Well, this sounded like a great place on your recommendation, so we decided to check it out for our club's future activities." He bought it. This guy was really stupid.

He said to come on in, and we did. The lobby was ornate with gaudy wallpaper and antique furniture. We went up to a desk with a woman seated at it, dressed in leather so tight it made her breasts pop up like grapefruit. Ralph showed his card, and she checked it against her book. She smiled and asked if Buck and I had cards. Ralph said he invited us in to look the place over. She smiled again and gave us cards that said we were guests and that we were limited to basic functions of the club as printed on the back of the cards. I looked and there wasn't much there. I didn't care.

Ralph asked if Wendy was available and was told she was free. He motioned to us, and we followed. We went into a small room, and after a few minutes an attractive woman came in and seemed a bit surprised by all of us in the room. I said to ignore us as we were just observing. She said, no problem, and went to Ralph. She must have known him as she started to undress herself. She looked at us, and I said we liked to watch. She said, whatever, and proceeded to undress Ralph. I had my pocket camera in hand and was quietly snapping pictures as they did their business. I looked at Buck, and he was just drooling. I had enough watching and had plenty of pictures to provide to any lawyer. We excused ourselves and went out quickly. We went out the front door and were heading to my car just as the same patrol car came around. He stopped and asked if I caught my little fish.

Dominatrix Murders

I said, "Hook, line and leather whips." I showed him the preview pictures on my camera, and he said to have Trapper send them to Detective Lawson, his buddy in Pontiac. They must have checked after I mentioned Trapper. I said I would. He thanked me and drove off.

Buck and I got back in the car and headed towards Fraser. Buck was still a bit charged up from watching the Dominatrix work over Ralph.

"Let's go to a strip club tonight," he requested.

"Buck, Penny would be crushed if we went on our own. She wants to go, too, and I said we'd set aside the time this weekend. Go home and work the steam out exercising," I said. "You know you can go by yourself if you really want to. I don't have to hold your hand."

"It wouldn't be as much fun without my posse with me," he lamented.

"Two more days, and we'll all ride out for action." I smiled. "OK?"

He said that would have to work, and we pulled into my office parking lot and went up to my office. I sat at the desk and fired up my computer as I pulled the SD card from my camera. I inserted it into the card reader and opened up the folder containing the pictures I took of Ralph. I copied them over to the computer and brought up the print program so I could make prints of them to show Elma. I ran off a copy of each picture, handing them to Buck as they came out. He sat snickering at them.

"You get them wet with drool, and you're going to pay for the paper," I joked.

"Elma's not going to like these," he said quietly.

"I know, Buck, but it has to be done, and there are still the deaths of his last two wives. I don't want Elma to end up on a slab in the morgue," I cautioned. "We get her away from him now, and it cuts his funds off. He'd have no reason to harm her."

"Or all the more reason to," Buck warned.

"Yeah, I had that in mind, too. We may have to lean on Ralphy boy a little, just to warn him what may happen to him should anything happen to Elma."

Buck grinned. "Can I beat on him a little?"

"We'll see," I said with a smile. "Now go home so I can go see Penny and take out my frustrations on her."

Buck got up and said he'd see me bright and early. After we all got back from Vegas, Buck went back to his job as security, watching cars. One day he had a run in with one of the owners of the security company and told him politely to shove his head up his ass. Buck quit. He didn't really need the job, it was just a bit of extra cash to spend on his classic cars that he restored. Buck was retired and on a nice pension from General Motors before they had money problems, so Buck had an income allowing him to bug me now. I had no problem with that. He was a big help to me, and he was scary looking. Great for intimidating suspects.

Buck said his good-byes and left. I just sat for a bit staring at the pictures that would either bring Elma's world crashing down or give her relief. I'd find out in the morning. I closed up the office, putting the pictures in my folder, and went out to my car. I drove home and found Penny in the kitchen trying to bake, I think. There was smoke everywhere. I thought the house was burning down at first.

"What in the world are you doing?" I asked, choking from the smoke.

"I was trying to bake cookies, but now we have charcoal briquettes for the grill." She looked so sad it broke my heart.

"I don't expect you to be a great cookie maker, I usually don't eat them anyway," I said, trying to comfort her. She dropped her head on my chest as we stood in the smoky room. "Let's open up some windows and go out to the backyard for a while."

"I'm supposed to have a baker on the show tomorrow, and I wanted to be able to say I could bake. I guess I won't say anything about my abilities to make hockey pucks."

We sat on the picnic table watching the smoke slowly stream out the windows, and I said to her, "What to see some dirty pictures?"

She looked at me strangely as I showed her the photos I took of Ralph. I had blurred out anything obscene on the pictures with the computer so as not to offend Elma. Penny turned the pictures this way and that and was studying them.

"Are you learning anything?" I asked.

"This girl looks familiar. I think she came with the dominatrix we had on the show the other day. I'm not certain, but the face is familiar." Penny handed me back the pictures. "And just what did you get into while at that club?"

"Not a thing. I just observed," I defended myself.

She sat there looking at me. "I guess I'll have to believe you. I may still check with Buck to see what he says."

Dominatrix Murders

"Buck wanted to go to a strip bar tonight. I told him he'd have to wait for the weekend."

"Is Elma coming in to see her husband being unfaithful?"

"Yep, tomorrow morning. I'm a little reluctant, but it has to be done."

"Maybe after about fifty or sixty cheating husband reports you'll get over the reluctance," Penny offered.

"I think that may help." I was silent for a bit, then it hit me. "Hey, the smoke made me forget about my big events of the day." I told her everything from the morning, down playing being shot at, to how I smacked Trapper with Marylou's hand, and how Weston was cleared of murder charges, then up to our trip out to Pontiac.

She grumbled a moment then said, "I really hope you don't get your fool head shot off now." She wasn't smiling. I kissed her cheek. "That isn't going to make it better," she grumbled again.

I said I'd be careful.

The smoke had finally cleared, and we ventured back into the kitchen. I picked up one of Penny's attempts at cookies and found I couldn't even break it in half. She started laughing while looking at her mess.

I said she could clean it up tomorrow. I had a few frustrations that needed tending to since I didn't get any action at the club. She asked if I still had the handcuffs handy. I said I did, but this time she got to wear them.

*

Chapter Eleven

I set my alarm extra early that morning. I wanted to get into the office early to get set up for Elma. Penny was still asleep and still handcuffed to the bed. I smiled. I got myself ready and then kissed Penny as she stretched awake, asking me to get the damn cuffs off her. I said I might just leave her like that. She glared at me so I let her loose. She got herself ready to go conquer the baking guests on her show. I asked if she was going to take one of her cookie creations with her. She gave me the one finger salute.

With clothes properly in place and our props in hand, we kissed on our way out the door. She drove off as I was getting my car started. I sat for a minute thinking about what was going to happen that day. I would be crushing a woman who had a decent marriage and sex till now, but I might be

Dominatrix Murders

saving her the heartache of his unfaithfulness and maybe even her death at his hands. If Ralph was actually a murderer. I was beginning to doubt it since he was so stupid.

I arrived at my office around 8:30 and found Buck plopped out on the lobby chairs. I kicked his feet again, and he came to life.

"Did you sleep here all night?" I asked.

He grinned and said, "Nope, got here about a half hour ago. I like to start my day bright and early."

I opened the door, and he went for the client chair and plopped there. I sat at my desk and checked my machine. I still used an answering machine instead of voice mail. I liked the control better with the machine. I warmed up my computer and brought up the video editing software then proceeded to make a DVD copy of the video that Buck recorded for me the day before. I was going to give Elma a copy and put one away for safe keeping along with the original.

My phone rang, and I checked the caller ID. It was Benson. "Hello," I answered.

"Jim, Dave Weston was let out this morning, cleared of charges of murder. Lincoln wasn't happy, but there was nothing he could do about it. Prosecutors talked extensively with Marylou

Martin early this morning and got her statement on record, so she should be safe for now. The media has already been hounding Weston, but we managed to keep Martin in the background. Her husband is still out of town, but she'll have some explaining to do when he returns. There's still the death of Noreen Weston. Police are looking into the dominatrix angle. They weren't happy with the mess at her office. I told them that's the way you found it. I still need your statement on record as to finding Martin. Get it to me as soon as you can." He finally paused and took a breath.

"I'll write up my entire procedures for my investigations and have them to you this afternoon. I'm getting ready for my cheating husband report. She's coming in this morning, and I'm bracing for it," I said.

"Good luck on that. Let my office know if she wants to proceed with divorce. We'll schedule an appointment for her. About the Weston case, submit your bill and I'll have a check cut for you today. You did good work. I'll definitely be using you again," he said, then said good-bye and hung up.

I looked at Buck who was watching me on the phone. "Weston was cut loose, charges cleared and so far all is well with Martin. They still have to find the murderer of Weston's wife. He or she is still out there."

Dominatrix Murders

Buck smiled and said, "They should put us on the case. We'd find them fast."

"I like your enthusiasm, but let's get through with Elma first." It was 9 a.m., and there was a knock at the door. Buck went to open it and found Elma standing there looking apprehensive. Buck was respectful towards Elma and quietly told her to come in. I got up, came around my desk, and pulled the client chair out for her. Buck went and sat at one on the chairs by the door. I sat at my desk, and I could see Elma wanted to say something.

"Elma, let me say this is never easy to give reports on spouses who wander." I hoped that broke the ice with her. She looked at me with eyes that said she knew. "We did some investigating of your husband, and I'm going to show you a video and some pictures that I hope you can brace yourself for." She nodded. "As you can already imagine we did find that your husband has been cheating on his vows. He freely admitted to me and Buck about his activities with a bondage club in Pontiac that fronts for a sex club. There was no other one woman involved, just his dalliances at the sex club. I think that would be enough, and our video and photos prove it. This is also evidence that you can use to proceed with divorce if you decide to go that far. Are you ready to see what we have?"

She nodded her head and quietly said, "Go ahead."

I turned the TV towards her and put the DVD in. It started up, and she sat quietly as the screen came to life showing Ralph and me at the pool store talking at the window. It ran, then ended. She was silent. I told her that we followed Ralph to the bondage club in Pontiac, and he had invited us in to watch during which time I secretly photographed Ralph with one of the dominatrixes. I took out the photo file and said I was going to show her only two, the rest were basically more of the same so no sense in dwelling on them. She said she wanted to see them all, and I handed the folder to her. She sat going through each and every one at least twice.

"Son of a bitch! The Bastard! I knew he was dicking somewhere else. I wasn't good enough for him! Couldn't get enough fucking at home, had to go get some stray pussy and bring home their diseases to me. I'll fry his tight little ass for this!" she spewed. I could see even Buck was a bit shocked by her outburst. Elma went on swearing for another minute then calmed down. She looked at me and blushed, saying she was sorry for the outburst.

I told her it was perfectly understandable.

"Elma, I have something else to cover with you, something important you may need to know. I had a friend of mine in the local police do a background check, and it seems your husband was married twice before. Did you know about this?" I asked.

Dominatrix Murders

She looked at me blankly and said, "He never mentioned any other wives, I was a bit surprised when he said that in the video. I assumed he was just making it up."

"No, he wasn't. You told me you had money. I assume you are well off?" She said she was. "Ralph's two prior wives were also wealthy, but after Ralph ran the money down, the wives mysteriously died. One by car accident and the other by suicide. My police friend says they suspected he was involved with the murders, but he came up with alibis to cover his ass. I'm not sure how Ralph is going to take to finding out you know about his running around. I would suggest finding a place to stay and tell him by phone that you know. I don't want anything to happen to you like what happened to his other wives. If he thinks you are going to divorce him he may act on it to prevent you from taking the money away. You may need protection." I looked at Buck and could sense he knew what I was thinking.

Elma looked at me for a minute and asked if I did protection work, I looked at Buck and he got up and pulled his chair over to us.

"Ma'am, if you'd like, I can provide you with protection till this whole thing goes away. My pleasure to help such a nice lady." He emoted such sweetness I could feel new cavities in my teeth growing.

She giggled. I knew she liked Buck from the first time they met at my door. She nodded and said, "Mr. Buck, I would love to have you provide protection for me. I will pay you well. Just keep that lying son of a bitch away from me."

Buck grinned and said, "Let's go confront the lying son of a bitch so you can tell him what you think of him."

She giggled again. "I'd like that very much." She looked to me and said, "Please have your bill ready for me, and I'll see you get paid right away. Thank you so much for your efforts."

Buck helped her up and asked her to wait out in the hall for him, that he'd be right out after he conferred with me. She went out and he closed the door.

"Buck, don't go getting her pregnant now," I joked.

"Shit, I have no intentions of getting anywhere near a bed with her, but she is a nice lady and I'll help her for a few days," Buck said.

"Just don't go getting yourself or Ralph killed. Call me if you have any trouble you can't handle, which is a dumb thing to say. You can handle yourself." I grinned.

Dominatrix Murders

He smiled and left. I just hoped she didn't kill him with kindness.

I sat back at my desk as the door opened again and a foxy brunette with a rack to die for stepped in and asked where the travel agency was. Damn. I told her, and she went out. I was going to have to go up there and see what the attraction was. It sure wasn't in my office.

*

Chapter Twelve

I opened up my diary on the computer, the one I have written in for over six years now. I may have missed a number of days, but it was pretty complete. If I needed to remember something, I could do a search and find the day it happened fairly fast. Most men would call it a journal, not a diary, too female sounding. I didn't care as long as I documented my day's activities. Since I was now over 60 and closer to senility, I needed to have something to help remember my past. I laughed. I wrote in what happened with Elma in detail and then shut it down.

I heard some noise behind me and turned to the window to see the weather had fouled, and it was storming out. Living in Michigan, you have to get used to changes in weather at any minute. It was pouring rain, and I was glad I had nowhere to go at the moment. The traffic in the street hadn't slowed with the puddles forming. Rain or snow, they ignored the mess. Michigan drivers like to push the edge when it comes to driving. They don't care who or what is in their way, just get there. I sometimes wanted to bitch-slap drivers who rode my ass trying to get somewhere, and then they would find an opening and whiz around me and down the road. I would have to laugh when I would get to the next light and there they sat, no further ahead, jerks.

Since it was becoming a day to stay indoors, I sat writing up my report for Benson, planning to drop it off later that day and pick up my pay.

About a half hour later, I turned to my door as it opened. In came Dave Weston. I was a bit surprised, and told him to have a seat, pointing to my client chair.

"Dave, what can I do for you?" I said.

"Well, first, I want to thank you for getting me off by finding Marylou or Cindy, whatever her name was." Sounded like he hadn't talked to her after they let him out. "I also want to ask a favor."

I nodded to him, and he continued. "I did love my wife, even if I was an insensitive bastard when it came to whoring around. Noreen was a good woman, despite her unusual occupation. She provided a need, and someone wasn't happy that she did. I think it was a city official, being protected by the police or at least one of them. I want to hire you to find out who murdered her."

He went quiet and looked distressed.

"I'm sure the police will do that for free," I said.

"Not if they're covering their asses, they won't. I want an independent investigation to get to the real culprit," he said. "My wife and I had a good deal of cash put away. It's all legal, and I can pay you whatever your fee to do this job - please." He looked like a man on the edge.

"If I agree to help you, you're going to have to be absolutely straight with me. I don't like being kept in the dark. That agreeable to you?"

He said it was, and then he took an envelope out of his jacket pocket and handed it to me. I opened it and found a thousand dollars in large bills. He said it was an advance. I told him he had just hired a P.I. and shook his hand.

"OK, may as well begin at the beginning. What got your wife into such a business?"

"Noreen was always into strange activities, Wicca, bondage, new age stuff. She felt she could save the world one person at a time. She got referrals through the local new age stores and then started to build up a clientele through personal referrals and word of mouth. She opened the office about a year ago, and it started slow but built up so fast that she had to limit her customers. She never got into sex. It was just a way for men mostly - a few women - to get rid of their frustrations from having to be the bad guy at work. In her office through the bondage, they were the underling, the bug that she could step on. They wanted the release of pressure from the weight of responsibility, and Noreen provided that." He went silent for a moment. I wasn't going to rush him. "Lately Noreen was acting strange, well... stranger than usual, and she was wanting more money for her work. I said she'd get too greedy and put herself out of business. She wanted more, and she wanted the power she was starting to feel over her clients."

I said, "Someone didn't like her pushing, you think?"

"Yeah, someone. I know Noreen kept a list with all her clients' names in it. I don't know where she kept it. She wouldn't tell me, said it was privileged information. She wasn't a registered therapist so that info wasn't really privileged, but she kept it hidden. She said to protect herself. She also kept videos of her sessions. She had a camera hidden on her back room that recorded them."

"I didn't see any camera when I was checking the place," I said.

"It's very well hidden, and the recorder is above it, over the ceiling tile."

"Can we go there and take a look at the set-up? With you there, it may make things easier."

He agreed, and we went out. The weather had changed again, and it was getting sunny out. We took my car, and I went by Benson's office first to drop off the statement and get my check. Then I drove over to Noreen's office. Dave was fairly silent the whole way over. We pulled up in front of the novelty store and went in to see Willy. He greeted Dave like an old long lost friend. Willy said he heard about Dave beating the rap, and Dave said that I was the one who got him off. Willy thanked me for helping. Dave asked Willy for the extra key since the police had his. Willy said that they went through the place, but he didn't think they found anything. He gave Dave the extra key, and we went down to the office and in.

"The camera is a tiny thing. She had it well hidden in the ceiling by a smoke detector."

We went into the back room, and he pointed to the smoke detector. I got up on a chair and looked closer at it. There was a small lens peeking out from the side of the thing. I asked where the recorder was, and he said to move the ceiling panel next to the lens. I did and found the small VHS recorder tucked in a hole in the wall. I went to pop out any tape in the thing but nothing came out. I flipped open the cartridge door. It was empty.

"Noreen or someone took the tape out. Do you know where she may have kept her collection of tapes?"

"I have no idea," was all he said.

"I don't suppose she told anyone about the recordings," I said.

"Hell, I didn't know she was doing it till I came in one day and found her up there changing tapes. She was pissed that I found out."

"Sounds like she was into more than just attitude adjustments. Maybe starting to blackmail some of her wealthier clients."

"Well, that would have gotten her killed easy enough." He grimaced.

I got down and continued, "We have to look more around your home to see if she may have a secret stash there. You mind?"

"No, let's go now. The cops have finished there, too, I hope."

We took the key back to Willy, and he said there were two more months left in the rent. Dave said after that he was finished with the place. We left and went to Dave and Noreen's modest little home in Roseville. We drove down Wallace Street, a quiet little road, just off Little Mack. The house was about one third down on the left. We parked and we went in. The place looked like it had been searched. Police are not known to clean up after themselves.

"Is there a particular room that Noreen spent time in more than others?"

"When she first started out, she used a small office in the basement, but the neighbors started to complain about the traffic coming and going to the house, so she got the office on Gratiot. The room is still down there, but the police pretty much wiped it out."

I was thinking that Lincoln probably enjoyed himself rummaging through that room. We went down to the room and as Dave said, I couldn't find much to go on. I walked around the basement examining the floor joists overhead looking for hidden panels. I checked the other small side rooms and the laundry room but really didn't see anything suspicious. I knew the water table in the area was fairly high and I asked if Dave had a sump pump. He led me back to the laundry room and pointed to the corner. There was a round hole in the floor about two feet across, and it had water in it. The sump pump was just at water level and was ready in case of flooding. I got out my pocket flashlight and looked into the murky water. Just behind the pump I saw a string attached to the side, going down into the water. I reached over, pulled it up, and out of the water came a small plastic container. I brought it out into the other room and set it on a workbench. Dave was amazed that it was there. I said my grandfather used to hide his chewing tobacco from my grandmother in the sump hole water in an old mason jar. That's why I looked. I examined the plastic container and said it looked like it was recently opened, the way it was still clean and not slimy from the water. I carefully opened the top. We looked in and found a key.

"Ah, ha," I exclaimed. "The mystery continues."

*

Chapter Thirteen

We were looking at the key when we heard a floor board creak above us. I quietly asked Dave if anyone was supposed to be in the house. He said no. I reached under my jacket for my Glock and realized I had left it in my desk drawer in my office. Some big shot P.I. I was, totally unarmed. I put the key in my pocket, and we went to the stairs. Just as we got there I saw a couple of baseball bats against a wall. I took one and gave one to Dave. I quietly went up the stairs, followed by Dave, and came out into the kitchen listening for any sound. Dave and I went into the living room and were heading down the hallway to the bedrooms just as someone came flying out of the first bedroom and ran into us. He had a ski mask on and was about my height.

I brought up the bat, and he rolled low, pushing into my legs, knocking me back into Dave. He sprang up just past us and ran to the kitchen. Dave was trying to get up and bumped into me trying to get up. It reminded me of a comedy routine as we followed after the intruder. He had gone out the back door and was climbing over the backyard fence as we came out. I just stood there, pissed at myself for being unarmed.

"I wonder what he thought he was looking for," I said. "The police would have just come in to look, but this guy snuck in, middle of the day, with his face covered, so no one could I.D. him. This is getting odd." I looked at Dave, "There's something that Noreen left behind that someone wants. We need to find it."

We went back in the house, and I took out the key and examined it closer. It was a Master lock key, so I said to Dave, "This is from a lock somewhere securing a door to keep people out. Do you know if Noreen had a storage unit somewhere?"

"None that I know of. We had one years ago when we first moved here from Lansing. We had it for about a year then took our stuff out of it when we moved to this house. Noreen said she was going to tell them we were done with it."

I asked where it was, and he said it was just off Masonic Road in Fraser. I knew the place, and asked if he remembered the unit number. He said it was number 78, and as far as he knew it belonged to someone else now. I said I'd check it later. We spent the next two hours going through his house, closets, attic, anywhere there might be things hidden by Noreen. We came up with nothing. It was nearly 5 p.m. and I said I had some business to attend to, just an excuse to get away for a while. I said I would start to do some serious investigating in the morning, and I would keep him apprised of my findings. He seemed happy with that, said he was tired and would rest. I told him to keep the baseball bats handy just in case, or better yet, if he had somewhere else to stay. He said he could go stay with his sister in Warren for a couple of nights if her kids didn't drive him nuts. I gave him my card with my cell phone number and told him to call anytime if he found or thought of anything else important. He gave me his cell number, and I put it in my Treo as he gathered some clothes to take with him.

I drove him back to my office to get his car, and he drove off. I went into the office and sat at my desk, playing with the key. I called a locksmith friend of mine I've known for years, although I hadn't talked to him in a while. He was surprised to hear from me, and we talked a bit about what we had been up to over the years. I told him about my present occupation, and he was impressed. I told him I needed some professional advice. He said, shoot. I told him about the key and described it, giving him the serial number off it. He looked in his book of locks and keys and said that was from a typical Master lock you'd buy in a hardware store, nothing special, just a bit more muscle than most locks but not impossible to open. I thanked him and said we had to get together to talk old times. I knew it wouldn't happen, but it sounded nice to say it.

I pulled out my local yellow pages and looked under storage. Found the one I wanted, Extra Space Storage, and called. A young sounding man answered and asked if he could help me. I said I needed to know if Dave or Noreen Weston still rented unit 78. He paused and asked if this had something to do with her murder, that he had read about it in the paper. I told him I was a private investigator and was looking into the case. He did some typing at his computer and said they didn't have that unit anymore. I asked if Noreen had rented another unit. He checked and said she hadn't. I thought of something and asked if he had a Noreen Black renting a unit. He checked and said there was one on his list, it was paid through the year and it was a small one, 5X8, unit 201. I got the tingle. I thanked him and said I would be in with her husband to see what she might have left, and hung up.

I wasn't going to call Dave that night to tell him the news. It might just somehow get out, and I didn't want anyone beating me to it. I was a bit run down and wanted to see Penny, so I closed up and went home. Driving there I wondered how Buck was making out with Elma and Ralph. I'd call him later to see. At least he hadn't called me to say he was in jail for killing Ralph. I finally got to the house and parked in my spot. Penny was at the door as I came up, holding a tray of cookies and looking proud.

"My God, you did it. You actually baked," I announced happily. She beamed and shoved a cookie in my mouth. I bit, and it was good. I'm not a sweets fan, cookies, cakes, I rarely ate all that kind of baked goods, but this was good. I tried to talk with my mouth full of cookie, she laughed and we went into the kitchen. She was telling me her baker guest on the show today explained the proper way to bake. I swallowed and said I had better not find an empty store cookie wrapper in the trash. She pointed to the mess on the counter and said she did it all by herself. We took the cookies to the couch after I got a glass of milk and sat. I only drank milk with cookies, donuts or peanut butter and jelly sandwiches. Otherwise, I didn't touch milk.

"How was your day, sweetie?" she asked. She smelled like pastry, so I started nibbling at her neck which usually drives her nuts. She pushed me back and said to talk now and munch later.

I told her about Elma and how she surprised Buck and me with her outburst after seeing the evidence. Penny laughed and said it was always the quiet ones that have the rage in them. I agreed. I told her about Dave Weston and our trying to find Noreen's hidden stash and my luck on finding the storage unit. She said it was too bad I couldn't shoot the intruder, next time I'd better remember to bring my gun.

"Rule number one! Always have your weapon, so you don't get killed," she insisted. "If he had a gun, you'd be dead now with a baseball bat in your hand. I'd have buried you with it, shoved right up your fool butt."

I was trying not to laugh with cookies and milk in my mouth but dribbled a little. She wiped my mouth with a napkin and kissed my lips. "Tasty," she said.

I took out my cell phone and told Penny I was calling Buck to see how his day went. After about four rings, Buck came on and said howdy.

"I'm demanding a raise in pay." He smiled through the phone.

"Take that up with Elma. She's got the bucks. Did you confront Ralphy boy?" I put the cell on speaker phone so Penny could hear.

"Oh yeah, we had a real nice little talk. I drove her to the pool store, and we called Ralph out to the parking lot where Elma ripped him a new ass. I was afraid I'd have to protect Ralph from her. He just stood there taking it all in and fearing for his life. He would look over at me every now and then. I'm not sure if he wanted help or wondered why I was there. She told him I was her bodyguard, and she wanted him out of her house immediately if not sooner, or she'd have me break both his legs. I was trying to keep from laughing. Elma and I left, and she got real quiet again. She asked if I was going to protect her till after Ralph was gone. I said I'd be around till she felt safe. That seemed to please her."

"Glad your day was good. I picked up a case from Dave Weston to track down his wife's killer. I'll tell you about it later. Right now I have some serious cookie eating to do. I'll talk to you tomorrow." We said our so longs and hung up.

Penny said that all the cookies were gone. I said that wasn't the cookie I had in mind to devour. She got wide eyed and ran to the bedroom. I yelled like Cookie Monster, "Cookie good, want cookies!" and ran after her.

*

Chapter Fourteen

I was dreaming of the Keebler elves baking me into a giant chocolate chip cookie and then I was about to be eaten by a giant when the phone rang. I stirred, reached over to the bed stand and grabbed my phone. I looked at the clock. It was 6:45 a.m. I answered grumpily.

"This better be important," I growled.

"Jimmy, it's Buck, I lost Elma."

I sat upright in bed. "You what? Is she dead or missing?"

"Missing. I was sleeping on the couch and had to use the john. I got up and went down the hall and did my business, came out and saw her bedroom door was open. I peeked in to make sure she was all right, and her bed was empty. I searched the house and checked the garage. Her car is gone. Man, I didn't expect her to fly the coop."

"She's a big girl. I just hope she went out for cigarettes and not to murder her husband. Just stick around and wait for her, that's all you can do. If she returns with a good excuse, tell her you quit unless she respects your job. Maybe that will work. If she isn't back by noon, call me." Buck said he would and hung up. Damn, what was she up to?

Dominatrix Murders

I plopped my head back down on the pillow but knew I wouldn't sleep.

Penny mumbled something about good cookies and rolled over away from me. She could sleep through a bomb blast. I was remembering when she was in the hospital recovering from her kidnapping by Waters and Morgan, and Trapper fired his gun twice to stop Alice Stone from killing me. Penny barely woke and just asked for some quiet. I would wake up when her stupid cat would jump up on the bed. I like cats, but her cat, Shadow, just seemed to be indifferent to me. I know cats are supposed to be indifferent to people but this one just plain ignored me.

My mind went back to Elma. Where was she? I should have asked Buck where Ralph was staying, and if Elma knew. She hadn't paid me yet for my services rendered, so I hoped she didn't get her fool head blown off. I still couldn't slow my mind down enough to sleep, so I got up, went out to the family room and flipped on the TV. It was just after 7 a.m., and the viewing was limited to morning shows with those teeth bright hosts and infomercials. I don't like watching the news, it's too depressing, so I put on the cartoon network and watched Bugs Bunny for the zillionth time. Him I can relate to.

Around 7:30 Penny came staggering out and asked what I was doing watching cartoons. I told her about Buck's call as she sat next to me.

"You think Elma is up to no good?" she asked.

"I haven't any idea," I replied. "I'm going to the storage place today and hopefully there will be some evidence to solve Noreen's murder in there," I said.

"Maybe you'll find Ralph's body in there, too." She grinned.

"Don't even joke about it," I replied. "Who do you have on your show today?" I asked changing the subject.

"I think there's a judo kung-fu kind of person on today. He's into meditation and all that stuff," she mumbled, still half asleep.

"I dread you coming home now. I'll either be kung-fu'd to death or forced into a lotus position on the floor."

"Lotus position is yoga, sweetie, not kung-fooey." She smiled and put her head on my shoulder.

We sat watching Elmer Fudd trying to avoid getting married to Bugs Bunny in drag. I love these cartoons. Penny drifted off again, and I had to shake her to go get ready for her hosting duties.

105

Dominatrix Murders

She stumbled off to the bathroom and came back out a half hour later looking fresh and awake and dressed. I wondered how she could do such a quick change. She went into the kitchen after giving me a kiss and got a couple pieces of toast and juice. I went to get myself ready for the day, and we met at the door, both heading out.

I got to my office around 8:50 and found Trapper sitting in the lobby. He grinned as I came up the hall and said he had to tell some babe in a mini-skirt where the travel agency was. I hissed and said I really had to go up and check them out.

In the office, I set up the new coffee maker I bought for my clients' pleasure and offered Trapper a cup. He agreed, and I got the thing started. I refused to drink coffee, but it was an extra feature of my office now.

"Don't they have enough for you to do at the precinct?" I wondered.

"I'm a lieutenant now. I assign work to everyone else and go hide." He laughed. "So you are on Weston's case now to find Noreen's killer?" he asked as he took the cup.

"I'm glad there is a pipeline for my business to the world, and I don't even twitter. Damn foolish thing anyway." I grimaced. "I could see me trying to twitter right in the middle of a shootout. One hand on my gun, the other typing furiously with my thumb."

"Any progress on the Weston case?" Trapper was curious.

I filled him in on everything that happened the day before, starting with Elma and on to our search of Weston's home and finding the key. Trapper laughed when I related leaving my gun in the office when we ran into the home invader. He said I should start sleeping with it. I said Penny might object to that. I asked if he had an hour to kill. He said he might and asked what nefarious plan I had in mind. I told him about the storage unit and asked if he wanted to go with me to check it out.

"You mean I have to work?" He laughed.

"No, just observe, I'll do the hard stuff," I replied. "I don't want Weston tagging along. I don't know if I can trust him for now."

"I'll follow you over in my car just in case I have to go do some real work," he said.

We went out, got in our respective vehicles, and drove to Extra Space Storage. The main gate was open so we drove in, and I cruised around the lot checking the numbers on the units until I found 201. Trapper pulled up behind me, and we got out.

Dominatrix Murders

"Well, this is it. Now to see if there's anything in here incriminating." I reached for the lock and stopped. Trapper came up beside me and saw what I saw. The lock was cut but hung to look like it was still together.

"Great, this just keeps getting annoying. I'm always a step behind someone." I tried the key in the lock to be sure it was the correct lock, and it opened. "Well, I have the right key anyway."

We pulled the rolling door up and went in. There were about four packing boxes and a small file cabinet, all opened and gone through. I picked up a couple of VHS tapes off the floor and read the label.

"She put the client number on the tapes but still no names. I hope the book or file she had those names in wasn't stored here," I said. We looked through the mess and then put everything back in boxes and the file cabinet drawers. There wasn't much paperwork, looked like just old files she put away. Trapper said we probably should call Lincoln and let him know this stuff was here since it was his case. I said I wanted to look a few tapes over just to see what I was up against. He thought that would be acceptable, we could take the stuff to Lincoln later. I think he just wanted to watch the tapes and get his kicks. We put the boxes in my car, and I was standing by the car looking around at the units when I noticed a camera housing down the end of the row and pointed it out to Trapper. He smiled and said we should go have a look at the videos.

We went into the small office at the front gate. There was a younger man at a desk. He smiled and said hello and identified himself as the manager.

"We need to see your surveillance tapes for the last couple days," Trapper said, flashing his badge.

"We only keep a week's worth, but you're more than welcome to have a look," the manager said. He got up and pulled out a box from under a cabinet with a huge TV sitting on it, showing the various areas of the yard watched by the cameras. He brought up six tapes that were marked by date on an erasable label. I asked if we could take them and return them later in the day. He said that would be all right, and I gave him my card. He asked if I was the one who called yesterday about the Weston case, and I said I was. He said it was funny because someone called just after me and asked the same questions. I cursed myself for not coming over right away. I asked if he had caller I.D. He said he did, went to his phone and looked up the backlog of calls, found the one from the time he remembered it came in, after mine. He wrote it down, I thanked him, and we went out.

"Can you see if you can find out the source of the number?" I asked. Trapper took the paper, went to his car and called someone, then waited as I put the tapes in my car.

He came to me with a big smile on his face. "Number is listed as Roseville Police."

*

Chapter Fifteen

"Crap!" I exclaimed. "This is getting deep. I can only think of one person on the Roseville police who would have anything to do with this case. Lincoln. Now, did he just think that Noreen would have a storage unit, or did he find out from someone?"

"Well, you're the P.I., you'll find out." He laughed. "Let's go back and watch some tapes."

We got back to my office. I set up the VCR, and we popped in the surveillance tapes and ran through them until we saw a car pull up to the unit in question. I slowed the tape down, and we watched a guy wearing a hoodie get out of the car and then pull out bolt cutters and snip the lock. The guy must have known that the camera was watching as he kept his back to it. He went in, and about twenty minutes later he came out with a number of tapes and a file folder, all of which he put in his car. He then closed the unit door, replacing the lock. He swung into his car and drove off. I re-ran the tape back to the beginning of his arrival, hooked up my computer, and copied the segment onto a couple of DVDs. I put the surveillance tapes in a bag and set them by the door.

"I have no idea who that was, but I got the plate number off his car. I'll run it and see who it's registered to, but I'll bet you a week's pay it's an unmarked Roseville police car," Trapper offered.

We ran through the client tapes, and after about three full tapes, we decided we had enough watching the weirdness. I was getting the picture of what Noreen's job entailed. The people in the videos weren't anyone we could identify. We saw no important people. I wondered if Lincoln got to the good tapes before us. The tapes were dated so if he couldn't find client names, he'd at least have known the tapes he wanted by the dates. I packed the tapes away back in the box.

Trapper said, "Want to go drop these off on Lincoln's desk?"

"Are you serious?" I asked.

"I got nothing better to do than to protect your ass." He grinned.

"OK, let's go stir the viper pit up."

Dominatrix Murders

We took the boxes out to Trapper's car, and then we headed to the Roseville police headquarters. I took two boxes, Trapper took two, and we went in to the front desk. Trapper plopped his boxes on the counter, flashed his badge, and asked for Lincoln, saying we found some evidence in the Weston murder. I could see that Trapper hadn't really changed since he worked Las Vegas police. He was still such a bad boy, he ate this stuff up. We were herded to a back squad room and into a small office where sat a man with a face so craggy he looked like a bulldog. He sported a close crew haircut and had a neck so thick it made his head look like it continued from his shoulders.

"Sergeant Lincoln, I'm Lieutenant Will Trapper, Clinton Township Police, and this is Jim Richards, private investigator, hired by Dave Weston to find his wife's killer," he intoned. "Jim came across some evidence while investigating that he thought you may need. I'm a good friend and just came along to help deliver these videos to you."

Lincoln just sat and stared. "I know who the fuck you both are. I do my job."

"Were you doing your job when the storage unit these tapes were stored in was broken into yesterday?" I asked bravely, only because Trapper was there.

"You got no proof I had anything to do with that," he replied coolly.

I took a chance. I pulled my cell phone out and dialed the number on the paper given to me by the storage manager. I heard the number ringing in my cell, then Lincoln's desk phone rang. He sat looking at it for a moment, then picked it up. I said hello, then hung up.

"That was the phone number on the caller I.D. given to me by the storage manager. A number that called yesterday inquiring about Noreen's storage unit. How did you know she had one?"

"I do my job, as I said. I don't have to answer to either of you. This is an open investigation that I'm conducting. Trapper, you're out of your jurisdiction, and, Richards, you pull no weight here," he snarled.

I dropped a DVD copy of the surveillance tape on his desk. "That's a copy of the video of the suspect and his car used in the storage break-in. Plates are easy to see. You may want to check them out." I was sure we all knew who they belonged to. I continued, "I'm not here to step on toes, I'm here to give you evidence for your murder case, just doing my civic duty. We brought you the tapes so they weren't stolen from Noreen's unlocked storage unit. There's too many crooks around nowadays."

"You'll do better to just stay out of my way, Richards. Hate to see anything happen to you. Understand?" He sneered.

Dominatrix Murders

Trapper leaned over the desk and quietly said to Lincoln, "Jim here is my good friend, anything happens to him, so much as a finger cut, I'll know who to look for. You understand, fat boy?"

Lincoln didn't want to start a scene, knowing what we had on him from the storage center. He just made his bulldog face as Trapper and I walked out. A couple of the homicide squad cops yelled to Trapper, saying hello to him. He recognized most of them and stood doing some small talk, occasionally glancing back to Lincoln who sat still glaring at his desk.

One of the cops leaned over and said under his breath, "Take that asshole with you, please." Trapper laughed and then introduced me, asking them to keep an eye out for me if I got in any trouble there. They all shook my hand and said they would. I gave them all my cards and said if they had any good cases they couldn't handle, I was available. They all laughed.

We went out to Trapper's car, and I just stared at him. "You're a real terror, aren't you? Captain Weber was right on with your crazy escapades from Vegas."

"You really don't know the half of it, and thankfully, neither did Weber." He grinned.

We swung by the storage center and dropped off the surveillance tapes, thanking the manager. I gave him my card in case anyone else inquired about Noreen's unit. I bought a new lock from his rack of storage equipment, and we went to put it on the unit. I would have to tell Dave about this later so he could decide what he wanted to do with it. Trapper dropped me off at my office. I thanked him for all the help. He said it was his pleasure, and he needed to go prove that he still worked in Clinton Township. He drove off, and I went into my office. Looking at the clock, it was just after 2 p.m., and I hadn't heard anything from Buck. I wasn't worried yet, but getting there.

I sat and took a breath, then made up a bill for Elma, hoping I could collect on it. After a half hour, I was getting a bit antsy about Buck so I called his cell. I got his voice mail. Damn, I hate that. I straightened out my desk and thought about calling Dave Weston to tell him about the storage. I picked up my desk phone and called his cell. It rang three times, and he answered.

"Dave, I found out Noreen had a storage unit rented under the name Noreen Black. I went there this morning with a cop friend of mine and found the unit was broken into. You haven't mentioned to anyone else about having a storage unit in the past?"

He was quiet, hopefully thinking, and then said, "I think that ugly cop assigned to the case asked me

Dominatrix Murders

all kinds of questions about Noreen's activities, and I think he did ask if we had one. Maybe I told him what I told you, I guess."

"That's OK, it's done now. I didn't find anything in the storage worthwhile, but maybe the good stuff was already removed. I don't know yet. I'll keep you informed as things change," I said and hung up.

I sat running through a few ideas I had on what to do next in regard to Noreen. I couldn't get anything from Lincoln. That was a door now shut. I should ask Dave what places Noreen got her referrals from and go from that angle. They might point me in a direction to the right people. I also thought about staking out Noreen's office to see if anyone else showed up looking for incriminating videos.

I was about ready to call Buck when my phone rang. It was him. I had a bad feeling about answering, but did.

"Speak to me, Buck. Give me some good news," I requested.

"Sorry, Jimmy, but the news is, Elma's been arrested for murder."

*

Chapter Sixteen

I was stunned. "Was it Ralph?" was all I could say.

"Hell, no. It should have been, but it was his Dominatrix that was killed," he said.

Now I was confused, but asked Buck where he was. He said, "I'm at the Pontiac police station where they are holding her. I called that lawyer guy you worked for. He sent one of his associates out, and they're working to get her out on bail. Good thing she has money, and luckily Ralph can't get to it. She has it all in an account he has no access to."

"Smart woman," I said.

"Not smart enough to stay home," Buck said.

"True. What happened?" I asked.

"I'm not really sure. The cops won't let me talk to her. I see the lawyer coming now. I'll call you back." He hung up.

Damn, two dominatrix murders in less than a week. Was this a trend? I wondered. I sat back thinking about Elma and hoping this was going to be a simple case. Buck called back about ten minutes later and said they did a quick arraignment and got her off on a half million dollar bond. She took care of it, and Buck was taking her home. I said to sit on her, and I would be there after he gave me the directions to her house. He did. I closed up the office and headed out.

I drove out to Troy, found the house off Sixteen Mile Road, and drove in the drive. Buck's mini-van was parked next to what I presumed was Elma's car, a Cadillac CTS. I went to the front porch just as Buck opened the door. He wasn't doing his usual smile. I patted him on the shoulder and asked where she was. He took me to her in the kitchen where she was sitting drinking coffee.

"Elma, what the hell did you do?" I asked.

I could see her eyes were red. She looked so sad, I went to her and gave her a hug. "I'm sorry. Can you talk about it?"

She nodded. "I made a mistake. I was just so pissed at Ralph, I wanted to really confront him and tell him what I thought."

"OK, tell me what happened with the Dominatrix."

"Around 1 a.m. I went to the motel where Ralph was staying, and when I got there I saw he was leaving. I followed him, and he went to Pontiac, to that club you said he belonged to. I thought that was great as I could catch him with his whore. He went in the front door. I went around the back and found a service entrance. I went in and found I was in a laundry where two women in grey uniforms were washing sheets. I snuck past them, peeked out a door to a hallway, and went out. I walked around. I guess everyone figured I was part of the place. No one stopped me. I looked in different doors and finally I found a room where I saw Ralph. He was yelling at the woman in leather. He was really mad and was screaming at her. I figured that was what they do till he grabbed her hair and pulled her to the ground. Then he pulled out a knife and stabbed her with it a couple of times. I screamed, and he saw me. He grabbed me and pulled me in. He pushed me on the woman, and I got blood all over me. Ralph took the knife, pushed it into my hand, and then ran to the door screaming that I came in and killed the woman he was with. The club security came rushing in and grabbed me and called the cops."

She went silent for a bit. I didn't push it. I looked at Buck, and he had the saddest face I've seen on him since I've known him. He felt bad for Elma something hard.

"Elma, how did you know Ralph was staying at that motel?" I asked.

"He called earlier in the day wanting some clothes. I asked him where he was, he told me, so I threw his clothes out on the lawn with Buck's help. Sometime later he got his stuff, but quietly. We didn't hear him," she replied.

"Where's Ralph now?" I asked.

Buck said, "I haven't seen him since they took him into interrogation. His ass is mine if I find him."

"OK, Elma, don't do anything stupid now. You are to stay in the house and don't leave it till you talk to the lawyers. I'll talk to them, too, and see what we can do for you. Just sit tight here, OK?" She said she would. I walked with Buck to the front door and said I'd be back tomorrow to see what we could do, for now just keep both eyes on her. He agreed, and I went to my car.

It was just after 5 p.m., and I headed back to the house. I was wondering what greeting Penny would have for me. Would I be forced into some oriental meditations or kicking out the walls? I got there, and the front door didn't open with her greeting me. I wondered what she was up to. I went in, and the house was quiet. I listened but heard nothing. I went out to the back porch and saw Penny in the yard, on a blanket sitting facing the lake. I quietly went out and came up to her, putting my hand on her shoulder. She gave a high pitched scream and grabbed my hand, twisting it around till I was on my knees and she was standing over me. I yelled, uncle, and she realized it was me and let up on her grip.

"What the hell was that?" I nearly cried from pain as I rolled on the ground. She tried to comfort me and apologized profusely.

"Sweetie, I didn't hear you coming up. I was meditating, and when you touched my shoulder, I reacted the way I was taught today. To protect myself."

"I'm happy you can do that without a gun," I said. "That hurt."

"It's supposed to, or it wouldn't be effective."

"You're a crazy woman." I grimaced. "I'm in pain here," I said holding my wrist.

"You're such a baby. I hardly twisted your arm."

"Hey, I'm a sixty year old male just at the peak of falling apart, and you want to disassemble me now," I lamented.

She started laughing and rolled back on the blanket. I took advantage of the situation, jumping on her, and she asked what happened to my falling apart. I said I would hold together long enough to take advantage of her. And I did.

Dominatrix Murders

It was good her back yard was bordered by a number of trees and foliage or we might have been arrested. All we did was frighten the wildlife. We gathered ourselves up, went into the house, and plopped down on the couch, our favorite respite. Penny asked me about my day. I told her everything, and she just sucked air about Elma and Ralph.

"What are you going to do about that?" Penny asked.

"I have an idea, but I'm going to need Trapper's help and his friend on the Pontiac Police. I'm going to call him tomorrow morning to get it started. Hopefully by afternoon we should be able to clear Elma."

I was still rubbing my wrist, and she pulled it over and kissed it. I asked how her show went. She filled me in and wanted to demonstrate some holds she learned, but I refused to be thrust around. She said we could watch the TiVo copy of her show, so we did. I was impressed by the way Penny handled herself learning the protective moves the instructor was showing. She was pleased with herself, too.

"I'll have to hire you out as bodyguard now," I joked.

She popped up and went into the kitchen, saying she was making Chop Suey for dinner. I groaned and asked if this was going to be an Oriental night at home. She said she rented two Jackie Chan movies to watch. I just gritted my teeth and said, great.

Around 7:20 my phone rang. It was Trapper. "I just got a call from Mike Lawson, homicide lieutenant out in Pontiac. He said Elma was arrested for murder this morning."

"How did he know to call you?" I asked.

"He talked to Buck when he came in to claim Elma, and Buck told him about you and your investigation into Ralph. Lawson remembered he had talked to a beat cop about the night they ran into you at the B&D club and you were throwing my name around. He is a good detective and can add two and two. He called me to see what I knew. I told him about Ralph's shady past, and he filled me in on the events of the morning. You think Elma could have done it?"

"I have my doubts, and I have an idea that may get a confession out of Ralph if I can get Lawson's cooperation and yours," I said.

He said anything to help. I said I would fill him in on it if we could get Lawson out there or on a conference call in the morning. Trapper said he would get Lawson to come there since Lawson owed Trapper a lunch. I said it worked for me. I hung up and sat gathering my thoughts on how to do my plan.

Ralph was so stupid, it might work.

*

Chapter Seventeen

I was up the next morning early, plotting my day and hoping Ralph was in good spirits. I called Trapper, and he said Lawson was agreeable to coming out. We could meet around 9 at Trapper's precinct. I asked if he could have a wire and a recorder setup for me and gave him a quick explanation of what I had in mind. He said it was good, and he would have a rig ready for me. I said that worked for me, and I would be there.

Penny was up and getting ready to go out to her show. I asked who was on today. She said, Marilyn Monroe. I paused and looked at her, not really wanting to ask but I did. She laughed and said Marilyn was part of a show that featured female impersonators who starred as celebrities, like Reba, Dolly, Cher, Joan Rivers, and more. I said there was a show in Vegas called La Cage, and it had that kind of entertainment. She said some of the performers coming were part of that show before it closed. I said that was interesting and too bad I couldn't come to see the show, but I had to go hook

Ralph into a confession. She wished me luck and headed out the door.

I got to Clinton Township precinct about 8:45 and was led to Trapper's office. Lawson was already there. We were introduced by Trapper and shook hands. Lawson was a huge, good-looking black cop, reminding me of Ving Rhames. About as bald, too.

"Trapper tells me you think you can get Flagg to confess to murdering the Dominatrix. You really confident that he'll fall for it?" Lawson asked.

"Well, the number of times I had contact with him, he was boastful and stupid. I think I can pull it off," I replied.

"He knows now that you were working for his wife to catch him fucking around. Think he'll trust you?" he asked.

"I'm sure I can work him. Like I said, he has a way of building himself up to be what he thinks he is, and, again, he's dumb as a board." I smiled.

"Well, it can't hurt to try. If we get him, all the better," Lawson agreed.

"Since the pool store he works at is within Clinton Township borders, I'll have an officer or two on hand to take him in custody till we can send him to you," Trapper said to his friend.

Lawson looked to me. "Do you really think he did it?"

"After I talked to her, I believe that Elma didn't do it, and Ralph has been under investigation for murdering his last two wives. I think it's a good bet."

"OK, let's take the fucker down." Lawson smiled.

Trapper had his people set me up with the wire, and we tested it just to be sure. Trapper said they'd sit on the side of the building where Ralph couldn't see them, and told me to say "Buck's a goof off" if I had any problems and needed help. I asked him, why that signal? He laughed and said, why not, Buck wasn't there.

"He wouldn't like that, but I'll use it." I laughed.

"If you remember, when I first brought you Ralph's background check, I said I wanted to be in on the bust of Ralph. Well, make me proud," Trapper said.

I went to my car and headed over with the rest following. The store was only about four miles from the station, so it didn't take long to get there. I arrived at the store. The cops came in from the K-Mart parking lot next door and drove up to the side of the place. Trapper waved to me, and I asked if they could hear me. He waved again. I was ready to go.

I took a big breath and organized my plan in my head, then I went in.

As I went through the door, I didn't see anyone, but then Ralph came out from the back room. He gave me a big salesman smile as he came up to me, then stopped when he realized who I was.

"What the hell you want?" he said.

"Ralph, hey, don't be mad at me. I was just doing a job. I came by to say I'm sorry. After I got to know you, I have a new respect for you."

He looked at me suspiciously, but had a curious expression, too.

I continued, "I heard what happened at the club in Pontiac. Must have been frightening for you."

"Hell, no, I wasn't frightened. Nothing frightens me," he huffed.

"Well, watching that girl die in front of you, knowing it could be you, wasn't that scary?"

"I was in control of the situation. I wasn't going to die," he replied.

I got in close to him and said quietly, like I was confiding in him, "You know, Ralph, I know what death looks like. I've shot a couple people in my life," I said as I pulled back my jacket to show him my gun. His eyes went wide, fixed on the weapon.

"Can I see it?" he asked excitedly.

"Oh, no, Ralph, I never let anyone touch my gun. It's my baby. Haven't you ever had a good weapon that was your friend?"

He circled around me looking like he had something to say but was reluctant to say it.

I went on quietly to him, as if I was sharing a secret, "I've looked into a man's eyes as I pulled the trigger once, twice, and watched the bullets impact in his chest. I watched the stun of death take over in those eyes, and it was such a rush. I imagine Elma must have had a taste of it as she plunged that knife into that girl's heart. Such a rush to be in that control over another human, eh, Ralph?"

"Yeah," he was breathing hard. "It is."

"You must have been real mad that night when Elma took control and stabbed that girl. Must have been real hard to watch it happen, Elma sticking it to her. But you wouldn't know that thrill of killing, the taste of blood. You're not that kind of guy, Ralph."

"I could be," he defended. "I could take a life, if I wanted to."

"Hey, Ralph, you're such a nice person. I'm sorry, but I just can't see you being a guy who could do that."

"I could!" he defended again. Then he caught himself.

"It takes balls to take a life, Ralph. Elma took that woman's life. You didn't."

He was getting wild eyed now. He was rubbing his face with his hands as if he was trying to remove the thoughts going through his head.

I pushed, "Elma had all the fun that morning, taking out her rage on that girl, plunging the knife again and again. And you just stood and just watched it happen, helpless to do anything."

"I wasn't helpless! I was in control! Elma wasn't in control. She just stood there and screamed in that puny pitiful way she has. I was in control! I know what it's like to take a life, I do. I've done it!"

"Nah, Ralph, you couldn't do something like that." I pushed more.

"Oh, yeah, I could and did. Elma didn't kill that girl, I did. I was so pissed at Elma, and I had to take my rage out on someone! I went to the club, and when that girl started her bondage shit, I just got so mad at people telling me what to do and that I was such a nobody. She pushed and pushed. I

129

couldn't take it. I got so mad, and I brought my little friend out, my wonderful knife, and I stuck her good with it. I felt the thrill of the life coming out of her. I was in control, I was! Then Elma had to stick her nose in, but I had an inspiration. Blame it on her. I could get everything if she was put away. I had the control!"

"Wow, Ralph, you got the balls. You actually killed that girl at the bondage club? Did you do in your first two wives, too?"

"You bet I did. They were just as bad as Elma with their pitiful little ways of making me feel like a loser, but I showed them all. I killed them, too. It took me a while to get them set up, but I killed them. I'm in control!" He was shaking with rage now.

I could see Lawson, Trapper and the two uniforms coming around the front of the building. I walked around Ralph, drawing his attention away from them.

"I'm the one with the balls!" he growled.

"Well, you'd better protect them where you're going to be shortly." I grinned.

He heard the front door open and glanced over. Seeing the police, he got a panic in his eyes, then turned to run. I stuck my foot out in front of him, and he went down. The two uniformed cops pounced on him, bringing him up and slapping cuffs on him as Trapper read him his rights. His eyes were just about popping out of their sockets as they dragged him out.

Lawson came to me, giving me a high five, and said, "Well done, my man. You were right, he is dumb as a board. I'm going to love beating him with the rubber hose." He laughed and went out.

Trapper smiled and said to me, "He's not kidding."

*

Chapter Eighteen

On my way to Elma's house, I got on my phone and called Dave Weston. He came on. "Dave, Jim Richards here. I need to know what places did Noreen get her referrals from for her clients? Can you make out a list for me so I have a place to start tracking down suspects?" He said he would have a list for me, and I said I'd stop by around noon. We hung up, and I pulled into Elma's drive. Buck opened the door after I knocked and looked at me hopefully. We went into the living room where Elma was lying on the couch looking miserable.

I handed her my bill and said, "You owe me big time, Elma. I got you off the murder charge. I tricked Ralph into confessing. Your lawyer should be contacting you about it and getting your bail back. Ralph still has to go to trial, and you'll need to testify, but he did confess, so it should be cut and dried."

Elma jumped up and gave me a big hug, thanking me. She took my bill, went to a desk, and wrote out a check for me. Buck asked how it happened, so I filled him in.

"Ralph is in jail in Clinton Township, but they'll be transferring him to Pontiac in a day or so. I would suggest you contact Mark Benson's office about starting divorce proceedings while he's incarcerated. Might be easier that way," I told her.

Buck looked at Elma and said, "Well, you won't be needing me now, I only worked a day, and I didn't do much good at keeping an eye on you."

Elma smiled, got her purse, gave Buck five one hundred dollar bills, and said he did fine, that she was just a pain in the ass. He bent down to her five-foot-two height and kissed her on the forehead, saying she was a fine person to protect. I told her that it would be good if she kept us informed about any developments with Ralph, in case of changes. She said she would and followed us to the door. Buck went to his vehicle, and I got into my car after agreeing to meet back at my office.

We drove off, and I hoped Elma would be all right now.

I got to my office and found a gorgeous brunette sitting on a chair in my lobby. I asked if I could help her, and she smiled and said she was waiting for her friend who was up in the travel agency. I swore to myself and went into my office, shortly followed by Buck who had to stop and talk to the beauty. He came in with a big grin and plopped his huge frame in the client chair, saying he thought that fox in the hall liked him. I just laughed and we sat talking about the events of the day.

Dominatrix Murders

It was then about noon, and I told Buck that I had to go get a list from Weston. I asked if he wanted to go. He declined, saying he hadn't been home in a day and a half and wanted to go freshen up. I said to stop back whenever, but to call first. He got up and went out. Passing the fox, he smiled, then went to his car. I called Weston, and he said that he had the list ready and would be at his house on Wallace.

I went out, locking my office. The fox was, sadly, gone. I headed over to Weston's house and drove up to find Weston sitting on the steps to his porch. He got up and came over to me holding out a folded paper. I took it and opened it to find a list of about six new age stores with contact names. A couple of them sounded like hard-core bondage supply stores. I would want those first.

"Are these the places Noreen frequented?" I asked.

"Yep, those are the ones that gave her referrals for her adjustments. I never spent much time in these places, maybe once or twice with her, but I knew she was getting help from them," he said quietly.

"Did you give this list to anyone else or tell anyone about these places?" I asked.

"Nope, only to you," he replied. I thought I would at least have a jump over Lincoln with these.

Although, since I believed Lincoln had something to do with the murder, he wouldn't care. I needed to get some names to narrow it down to Lincoln or someone higher up.

"I have a question. You mentioned you had children. Where are they?" I asked.

"My parents came and took them to their home for now. They live in Port Huron. It's hard on the kids. I'm going up to see them this week. I think it would be better for them to stay up there till this is all over," he said without expression.

I thought, being fifty miles away would isolate them from the crime and attention here, but Weston still had to deal with telling his children that Mom was not coming home anymore. That has to be something no father should have to bear.

I gave him the keys to the new lock on the storage unit and told him the number. The unit was cleaned out of any evidence so he could use it if he wanted. It was paid to the end of the year. He said he might go sleep in it and laughed sadly. I said I would be in touch and left him standing on his front lawn, looking miserable. The guy's world was crumbling. At least he still had his kids.

I drove over to Twelve Mile Road, then to Gratiot Ave. and down towards Eight Mile Road where the first store was located. A place called the Purple Pit, it was a head shop and new age store, and it was the closest to me at the moment. I had to drive around the block a number of times before I spotted the store. Duh, I should have seen it painted all purple and sporting the huge peace sign, made popular in the sixties by the head culture. I navigated the drive on the side, a narrow twisty path that led to a small parking lot in the back. I guess they didn't expect a lot of business. I got out of my car and walked around to the front, passing some guy spread out on the empty lot next to the store. At first, I thought he might have been dead, but he opened his eyes and asked if I had a buck for food. I could see his eyes, drug addled. Food was not on his mind. I said I was sorry but I was broke, blame the economy. He lay back and passed out again.

I came around the front of the store and went in. It took me back to my days in the sixties as a newbie hippy, smelling the incense and adjusting my eyes to the black lights making the posters glow in that odd blue light. I remember hanging out at the teen dance club, the Crow's Nest East in St. Clair Shores, watching great bands like the MC5 and Amboy Dukes featuring Ted Nugent. I sat with Bob Seger one night after his band the "Bob Seger System" rocked out the house. We talked about nothing in particular, but I was thrilled. The Strawberry Alarmclock and...well, I could go on but I was jumped on by an oddly attractive young woman as I stood entranced by the sights.

"Hey, man, can I help you?" she asked in a squeaky voice that I loved to hear, a child-like but giggly adult tremor that just made my ears perk up. She was attractive in an odd sense, not beautiful, but innocent, with a young, soft face that just needed to be kissed. I resisted. I looked closer and realized she wasn't that young, maybe in her forties. I was intrigued. She had metal piercings adorning her lips, nose and eyebrows. I wasn't fond of piercings, but she seemed to make them work. She wore black leather that covered her body, and she wore the spiked bracelets and collar that completed the outfit.

"Hi, I'm looking for Lorelei. Is she in?" I asked going by the list names of contacts.

"Wow, I'm Lorelei. Are you looking for an adjustment?" she asked, all bubbly.

"Beg your pardon? What kind of adjustment do you offer?" I asked.

"Massage or bondage," she offered. "What are you into?"

"Neither," I answered. She looked disappointed. "I'm interested in any information about Noreen Black."

She recoiled at the statement. "Why are you asking about her?" She squinted her eyes as she spoke.

"I'm sorry, I'm an investigator and I'm trying to track down her killer." I took out my I.D. and showed it to her. She took my I.D. case and badge and walked away. I followed. She stopped and looked at me and then at my picture and back to me. She gave me my case back and asked what did I want to know.

"Did you supply her with names of clients she may have helped in her business?" I inquired.

She squinted again and said, "Names of people that would curl your hair. Follow me." I did.

*

Chapter Nineteen

She took me to a small room off to the side, through some beaded curtains that were popular in the sixties. She turned and said in a low voice, "What's your interest?" I told her I was hired by Dave Weston to find out who killed Noreen. She smiled and said, "Noreen came to us here, and we supplied her clients that were looking for, as Noreen put it, attitude adjustments. I loved that term. They didn't want to say they wanted to be tied down and whipped, made to be submissive,

138

made to beg for their mommies, but that's what they wanted," she rattled out. "They were strange folks who didn't want to be recognized, but I recognized a few of them. Important people in the community, political people who I'm sure don't want their constituents to know they are into kinky stuff." She giggled.

"Like who?" I asked. She started to open her mouth to speak when the front door bell tinkled. She closed her mouth and walked out of the room. I stood back, looked out through the beads, and saw someone I didn't want to see, Detective Ben Lincoln. Now what the fuck was he doing here? I watched him as he briefly chatted up Lorelei, then I saw him move his hand back to where his gun was. I didn't want to shoot him, although the idea was something I liked, but not today. Lorelei was busy chatting as he put his hand on his weapon. I burst out from the back room.

"Well, well, Detective Lincoln, how nice to see you again." I had my hand in back of my jacket by my gun, just in case. He looked stunned and pulled his hand away from his weapon. I did likewise. I came up to the two of them. Lorelei squinted at Lincoln.

"You are a police officer or a private investigator?" she asked of Lincoln.

Dominatrix Murders

"I'm a police detective, ma'am. I'm investigating the murder of Noreen Weston. Do you know of this woman?" he asked politely.

Lorelei stood for a moment, then said in a calm voice, "Sorry, officer I don't know the woman, can't help you."

He looked at me. "You checking this out here, too?"

"Yep, and I got the same answer. Looks like a dead end here. Are there any other places that we may meet at today?" I asked.

His lip snarled, and he said, "I hope not." Then he said thanks to Lorelei and went out.

Lorelei watched him go and looked at me. "He's a bad one. I know who he is. I just pretended not to know him to throw him off. He knows a few people who used Noreen's services."

"I'm wondering if you might be in danger. You think maybe you should lay low for a while?"

She had been standing behind the counter all this time and suddenly brought her arm up. In her hand was a sawed off shot gun. She smiled at me and said she wasn't stupid. I had to agree.

She replaced the shot gun in its holder under the counter then looked at me and said, "You have a nice aura about you. Do you practice any kind of metaphysical arts?"

"I occasionally worship the gods of barley and hops, but that's about it," I replied.

She smiled and said, "Ah, a beer worshiper. I like that. I indulge in the brew myself on occasion. I don't like my senses being messed with, but every so often I like to climb to a higher level of consciousness." She giggled.

"I usually end up in an unconscious state. Back to Noreen, can you name a few people for me that I might want to talk to about Noreen's demise," I asked.

"We don't keep records of people's names. We just refer them to Noreen, or did refer, and give them a card." She picked up a card from a holder on the wall and gave it to me.

"You said you recognized some people, who?"

"Well, a certain councilman from here in town was one person I remember. His initials were F.R., and that's all I can tell you. It's a matter of confidentiality with our clients. He's someone you can start with." She winked as the front door opened again and a not quite elderly woman walked in. "Hello, Mrs. Webb, how are you today?"

141

Dominatrix Murders

"Fine." The woman said and didn't want to look at me. She turned towards the front of the store and went to a rack of leather goods.

Lorelei smiled and said quietly, "You can never judge a book by its cover. That woman is into kink with her husband. She's in here every other week looking for new toys."

I just shook my head and thanked Lorelei. I gave her my card and said if she remembered anything else that might help, to call me. She looked at the card and said she would do that. I went out to my car, now finding the guy lying out in the back parking lot. He raised his head and asked again if I had a dollar for food. I went to my car, took out two candy bars I had on the front seat, and tossed them to him. I said, enjoy, got in the car and drove off as he gave me the finger.

I drove out Eight Mile Road, the northern border of Detroit, and over to Woodward Avenue, up to a small store front called "Leather and Lace." I parked and went in to find three women all in black leather from full cover to skimpy bustiers. They had the whole Dominatrix package going for them. One came over to me and purred. "Hi, handsome, you come to play?"

"I'm looking for Mistress Terry. Is she in?" I asked.

The woman smiled and said, "I'll go get her." She slinked off to the back room and after a few moments, another woman appeared. I was a little surprised. It was the same woman who was on Penny's show this last week. She came up and asked if she could help me.

I took out my I.D. and showed it to her. "I'm wondering if you know a Noreen Weston. She also goes by Noreen Black."

"Is this about her murder?" she said quietly.

"I'm investigating for her husband, yes."

She motioned to me to follow her. We went into the back room, and she asked me to sit on a chair by her desk. I did.

"I saw you on Penny Wickens' show the other day. Penny and I live together," I offered to ease the conversation.

"Oh, so you're the P.I. she talked about. I was impressed by your exploits in Vegas." She smiled demurely.

"I'm sure Penny exaggerated a few details." I grinned.

"Oh, she had very nice things to say about you." She leaned forward, put her hand on my knee, and almost exposed her breasts.

143

I fidgeted a bit then asked, "About Noreen, did you know her?" She moved her hand back and looked off into the darkness of the back room.

"Noreen used to work for me years ago, before she married Weston. She was a prize pupil of mine. I trained her well. Then she decided to go off on her own. I had no problem with that, there are plenty of people out there to keep all of us Doms busy," she said.

"Did you supply her with referrals for her business?"

"Well, we weren't sending people to her, we have our own business to worry about, but occasionally we would turn a customer on to her if they lived near her. As to whom we sent to her, I couldn't tell you, just plain folks who liked to walk on the wild side. Do you think it was a client of hers that did it?"

"I'm exploring that avenue since her husband has an airtight alibi for the night she died. Do you find in your business that clients can get a little carried away or violent?" I asked.

"The people who come here to get their butts smacked all have a little bit wrong with them. Do you think being strapped down or chained up and subjected to humiliation is something normal, Mr. Richards?"

"Call me Jim, please. No, I don't personally think it's normal at all, but I believe this entire world is filled with people who have little secrets and odd behaviors that would shock their friends and families if they knew."

"Tell me, Jim, do you have any little secrets or odd behaviors that would shock me?" she asked coyly.

"Well, every third Sunday I dress up as Madonna, complete with pointy breasts, and do a dance to the moon." I grinned.

"Don't tease, I was serious," she said.

"Well, all seriousness aside, I'm not at liberty to discuss my peculiar habits. Penny is the only person I confide to in that regard." I grinned.

She smiled and said, "Lucky woman."

*

Chapter Twenty

Mistress Terry didn't have much more to offer, so I thanked her and went back to my car. I sat looking at the other addresses and then my watch. It was almost 4:30, and I was wearing down. Since I started my P.I. business, I had been missing taking the naps that old people like me take in the afternoon. I was getting too much exercise running around playing detective to worry about naps. I slept well at night, better now that I was wearing myself down during the day. I drove up Woodward to Fourteen Mile Road and all the way out to Harper Avenue. I cut around to Jefferson and up to our house.

I pulled into the drive, wondering what to expect tonight, and as I got to the door, Marilyn Monroe answered. I was a bit stunned as she breathed out, "Come on in, big boy," and did a little Marilyn squeal.

I was mystified. I knew it was Penny, but she did her make-up so well, it looked like Marilyn. She took my hand and pulled me into the living room. She had on the same tight dress that Marilyn wore in "Some Like it Hot," that gold number when she sang and danced. She was stunning in it.

"Did you kidnap my Penny and replace her?" I laughed.

She stayed in character as Marilyn and said, "Well, big boy, I am replacing your gal for the night. Are you pleased?"

I had to be careful answering that loaded question. "Well, I really am faithful to my Penny. But if she approves, you can stay for a while." I waited to see what reaction I would get. She squealed again, rubbed her hip against my private area, and giggled. She shimmied over to the TiVo in the tight dress she had on, came back, pushed me to the couch, and cuddled up next to me. This was so weird, but enjoyable. She flipped the remote on the TiVo, and we watched her show with all the female impersonators. In one segment, they made up Penny in the Marilyn make-up and dressed her. She was really good at the impersonation, as I could see sitting next to me. The show ended, and she blew in my ear. I looked at her and asked what was on her mind.

"Well, before I take all this make-up off I thought you might like to go down memory lane with me." She stood and took my hand, and we went off to the bedroom.

About two hours later, I staggered out to the kitchen and got two beers out of the fridge then came back to the bedroom. Penny was still in character, but her make-up was suffering a bit. I handed her a beer, and we cuddled.

"You know what?" I asked. She said, what? I said, "I love you."

She smiled and pulled me tighter to her with her arms around me. "I love you, too. As me, not Marilyn. Although if Marilyn knew you, she would love you, too."

I was getting real comfortable when the phone rang. I grumbled over to it and answered.

"Jim, it's Trapper. I just wanted to fill you in on the progress of our buddy Ralph. He was transferred to Pontiac this afternoon and is up on first-degree murder charges for the Dominatrix and a couple more for each of his two wives. Lawson threatened him with the rubber hose, and he sang like a bird. He was denied bail and the trail starts a week from Monday. Elma is going to have to be there as a material witness. Can you or Buck get her out there safely?"

"I'm sure one or the other of us can. I'll call her later to let her know. Just tell me what time and place, and we'll see Ralphy boy go down in flames."

Trapper gave me the details and said that Elma might have to sit around most of the day till they could get to her. I figured Buck would be good for it. I needed to work on my own case and wanted to be free. I said I'd call Buck and get him set up on it.

Trapper asked how my case was coming. I told him about my day and running into Lincoln at the head shop. He said it was good I was there. The woman might have been a victim of a fake robbery gone wrong. I said I believed Lincoln would have shot her to be sure she never talked about Noreen's clients. I said I thought we convinced him she knew nothing about Noreen's activities so she would be safe. Then I asked Trapper if he knew a council member in Warren with the initials F.R. He said it sounded like Frank Ropiello. I told him that was a person referred to Noreen by the Purple Pit. He whistled and said that would be a blow to his career if that got out, but how did it fit in with Lincoln? I said that was what I was going to find out tomorrow. He said, good luck, then said he had to get back to real police work and hung up. I wasn't bothered that he didn't say good-bye now that I knew why.

I came back to Marilyn, and she had a DVD on the bedroom TV, "Some Like It Hot" with her alter ego. I laughed, and we sat back and watched.

"Are you going to do this again?" I asked.

"Only if you can look like Brad Pitt." She giggled.

"Oh, well, it was fun while it lasted."

149

Dominatrix Murders

Later, after we had a late dinner, I told Penny about my day, the exciting visits to the Dom stores and how I ran into Mistress Terry. I told Penny that Terry tried to get frisky with me, but I held her off. Penny just snorted air and chuckled.

I called Buck and told him about Elma needing to be in court, and I said I'd pay for his time if he could play bodyguard again. He said that would be fine with him, but he didn't want me paying for his time, Elma gave him more than enough money for watching her. I said that worked for me, and I gave him the details. After that, I called Elma and told her what was happening then asked her if she got hold of Benson's lawyers about the divorce. She told me what they had planned. I said it sounded good and wished her well.

Penny and I both were a bit wiped out so, since Penny had washed away Marilyn, we decided to forgo our usual nightly exercises. We cuddled and went to sleep.

Morning came fast, and I staggered out of bed and to the bathroom. Penny had already gotten herself up and ready to go for the day. I wished I had her energy in the mornings. She kissed me and went off to work, saying she had a child psychologist on today. I thought that was something I had no fear to come home for. Children were not in our plans. Both of us were too old, and Penny was unable to have children. I got my body ready and dressed and checked the phone book for Warren City Hall. I added it to my Palm and headed out.

I drove over listening to the radio, being annoyed by all the commercials. I got to hear half of Bob Seger singing "Hollywood Nights" and cursing program directors as I pulled into city hall parking. I went into the building and asked the girl at the counter where Frank Ropiello's office was. She asked if I had an appointment, and I said no. She got on the phone and called, then asked what it was in regard to. I said it was about Noreen Black. The girl wouldn't know about Noreen Black as the papers all had her listed as Noreen Weston, but Frank Ropiello would know the name. She asked me to wait. After a minute a man appeared at a door off the side and waved to me to follow him. We went down a long corridor and into a plush office. He closed the door and motioned me to sit.

He sat looking at me. "So how much is this going to cost me now?"

"I'm not sure what you mean," I asked.

He just stared. "Aren't you here to collect your blackmail money?"

I took out my I.D. and showed him. "I was hired by Dave Weston to find out who killed his wife, not to collect anything from you." He was quiet, and I continued, "You know her as Noreen Black as I understand. Is that correct?"

He was quiet again, then, "I had nothing to do with her death and I don't know who is continuing to blackmail me. I have been paying some thug for the last two weeks, and I thought you were here to collect. I thought when Noreen was killed, God rest her soul, it would be over. I'm still being harassed by someone demanding money. First, it was Noreen doing the blackmail, now someone else has taken over."

I was really curious now. "Do you know a Ben Lincoln?"

He looked a bit shocked and said, "Yes, I know the son of a bitch. He was harassing me about Noreen's murder. Asking questions about who else was involved with her business. I'd like to know how everyone finds out I'm a client," he growled.

Lincoln beat me again. I needed to move faster. "I can't tell you how he knows. I'm not in his confidence. Do you think he may have been involved in her death?"

"I wouldn't put it past him. He was very anxious to know if I knew where Noreen kept her list of names of her clients. I said I had no idea, and he threatened to expose me if I didn't find out. How the hell can I know where she kept her information? I only went there a couple of times."

"Well, someone knows who her clients are. He or she is blackmailing them." I didn't see any reason to bother this man further, so I apologized and said he should talk to the police or he'd be drained dry. "But during my investigation, I'll see if I can find anyone blackmailing you." I thanked him, gave him my card and left.

*

Chapter Twenty-one

As I was walking out of city hall, I was shocked to see Lincoln coming up the sidewalk, not seeing me. I stopped and he saw me and stopped. We stared a bit, then I said, "Sorry, Frank Ropiello doesn't really know who any of Noreen's clients were. I beat him within an inch of his life, but he couldn't tell. Just wanted to save you the time and trouble. Later, somewhere else." I walked away, smiling. I could hear him swearing under his breath. I didn't look back.

I was really beginning to have the feeling Lincoln didn't murder Noreen. I couldn't put my finger on it, but it didn't jell. He really was just stupid, but then again, Ralph was stupid and a murderer. I drove out of the parking lot and saw Lincoln getting into his car. At least I saved Frank the agony of putting up with Lincoln. I drove out to the next address on my list, one in Royal Oak, and finally found the "Dom Shoppe."

The interior of this place was a little more film noire and dark. It had an evil feeling to it, and the women were all made up with pale skin make-up, looking more like vampires than Doms. With all the big deal over the "Twilight" vampire movies and books, I could see they were cashing in on the fatted calf. One of the undead women came up to me and hissed, "May I help you?"

I flashed my I.D. and badge rather quickly, hoping she would think I was a cop, and said I wanted to see Elvira. I didn't like the use of the name of my favorite "Mistress of the Dark," but I was sure this one wasn't even close to the original. I was wrong. After the first vamp went to get her, she came out in an oh so tight black dress that revealed ample bosom down to her navel. Her hair was jet black, straight and down to her voluptuous ass. She slithered up to me and asked if she could do me.

"Could you do me or what can you do for me?" I asked.

She said, "Either way, what would you like?"

"Well, I'd like world peace and a million dollars in my bank account, but I'm here to discuss Noreen Black or Noreen Weston, whichever you knew her as," I said.

She took on a quick flash of sadness and asked me to follow her. She was all proper and refined as the Queen of the Dead should be until we got to the back room.

"OK, what do you want from me, cop?" she spit out.

"I'm not a cop. I'm a private investigator hired by Noreen's husband to find her killer. You know anything that could help?"

"I'm tired of talking to cops. I told them everything I knew about Noreen. She came in occasionally to get some paraphernalia for her place, and we would talk about business." She turned away from me and looked distressed. Way too distressed for a casual acquaintance.

My tingle was buzzing, and I played a card. "You two were more than just business associates. How close were you to Noreen?"

She was silent, then, "I loved her. I'm not ashamed to say, she was a soul partner to me. We clicked. She tolerated her husband, but she was definitely not as straight as he would have liked it. We spent many evenings together."

I was a bit taken back by her candor. Surprised that Dave never said anything, or maybe didn't know.

"Noreen first came in here back when she went out on her own from Mistress Terry. I saw a young, innocent, yet determined, woman beginning her life as a real Dom. I got close to her, coached her, and loved her when she was willing." She went silent again.

"When was the last time you saw her?"

"A week before she...was killed," she choked out. "If you find the bastard who did this, bring me his balls."

"Do you know any of her clients? I'm trying to narrow it down."

"She had a number of influential clients, most of whom wouldn't want their kinks played out in public. If one of them found out about the others, it would be a disaster. I taught Noreen to be real careful of her client list, that it was precious, sacred. She wouldn't let that information slip out no matter what. I think that is why she was killed."

"Wouldn't you be in the same danger she faced with your client list?" I asked.

"I'm constantly surrounded by my women, and I'm rarely alone. It would be a lot harder to get to me." She smiled. "Noreen was alone out there. I didn't like it and tried to convince her to join me, but she enjoyed the freedom."

"Did you know she was starting to blackmail her clients?" I had to ask.

She gave me a dirty look like I had sworn at her, and said, "Noreen would never, ever do something like that."

"I have a city official who claims she was doing just that to him, and now that she's gone, someone else is continuing to blackmail him. I'm not trying to put a bad light on Noreen, but the evidence is out there."

Elvira was quiet for a good long time. I said nothing.

"Did Noreen say anything about taking on an assistant or helper?" I asked.

"Yes, she did mention about a month ago that there was a young girl hanging around her business, and she was thinking of taking her in since her business was getting so hectic. I think she said her name was Melody. Yes, it was Melody Williams, she said. Noreen wanted to train her to be able to handle the overflow, and I told her to be careful who she trusted. This is a cut-throat business." Elvira choked on that and began to tear up. I grabbed a tissue from her desk and gave it to her. She thanked me.

"I'm sure if Noreen was blackmailing any of her clients, she wouldn't tell you. Do you think Noreen was capable of doing such a thing?"

"Noreen was competitive and determined to succeed. She was a kind person though. I don't believe she would do such a thing."

"Maybe someone who knew her clients might have used her business to do the blackmail. Would that be possible?"

"Of course, people don't want their fetishes exposed to the world. We run a risky business of exposure which is why we have to guard our client's anonymity, and they have to trust us. Anyone knowing Noreen's business list could easily blackmail people." She wiped her eyes and sat up tall, looking defiant. "I hope you find out who is doing this so I'll know that my Noreen would never have stooped so low to blackmail her clients."

I said that I was finished and thanked her. She stood and walked me towards the front door. She came out of the back room and assumed her Queen of the Dead posture. At the door she whispered to me to let her know what I found. I said I would. Then I asked one last question, if she knew a Ben Lincoln. She said she didn't. I went out.

I sat in my car across the street from the store. I was thinking and watching to see if Lincoln would pop up. I wrote down all the information Elvira gave me. A new name in the case now, Melody Williams. I would need to find her. She could be the link to the blackmail and the murder. I thought about the videos that Noreen made of her sessions. Why, if she wasn't blackmailing her clients, would she tape them? And where was the damn client list? I took out my phone and called Weston.

"Dave, a couple of questions, do you know a Melody Williams?" I asked when he came on. He said Noreen mentioned hiring an office girl, but didn't say if she had or not. She said her name was Melody. I continued, "Do you know how to find this Melody?" He said no. "OK, one more question. I asked you to be totally honest with me when I agreed to take your case. The question is, did you know your wife was having an affair with a woman?"

He went silent for a bit, then I heard him sigh. "I sort of knew she was. She never came out and admitted it, but she spent a lot of time with a Dom named Elvira, and she always came home looking like a woman does when she's fucking around. I didn't push it. Maybe I should have, but what would that do? She'd get all pissed at me and maybe even leave me. I didn't want that."

"OK, thanks for the honesty. Now, do not, I repeat, *do not*, tell anyone about Melody. You hear?" I ordered.

"I won't," he said. I said I'd let him know what I found and hung up.

Now to go on a hunt for the missing link.

*

Chapter Twenty-two

I went back to my office. No beauties in the lobby. Oh, well. I checked my answering machine. Nothing. I just hate days where you have no mail, email, messages or visitors. Just makes you feel so lonely. I sat at my desk, took out the area phone book and looked under Williams. Of course there would be a dozen or so. I checked the areas they lived in and wrote down the numbers for the ones in Roseville. I'd start with those. I was beginning to feel that some cases could be a lot of nothing, just checking facts and spending time on the phone. It wasn't this way in the mystery novels I read. Well, maybe the "in Death" books where Eve Dallas was always running around interviewing suspects and digging through tons of possibles. Of course, she had super computers to gather the facts for her. I was born too early.

After about an hour of calling names and getting nowhere, I dialed a number in Sterling Heights, and a woman answered.

"May I speak to Melody, please?" I asked.

"She's not here right now. May I take a message?" the person asked.

"Do you know when she'll be back?"

"She went to work. She didn't say when she would be back." The woman seemed pleasant, so I pushed on.

"Has she started her job with Noreen Black?"

"I think she mentioned that name, but I couldn't be sure. It's in some office on Gratiot, in Roseville, a small consulting firm she said."

"Are you related to Melody?" I asked.

"I'm her sister. Just who are you, may I ask?"

"I'm sorry, how impolite of me. I'm with an agency that does background checks of prospective hires for employers. We make sure the people they're thinking of hiring are who they say they are. I hope you understand?"

161

Dominatrix Murders

"Oh, yes, I do. I've worked with a few people who should have been checked. They turned out to be not so nice people and messed over my employer. Do you have any questions I may answer about Melody, if I can do that?"

"Sure. Your name is?"

"Barbra, like in Streisand, and everyone calls me Babs, too," she replied.

"Well, Babs, what is your sister like as a person?"

"Very dependable, she never misses work, and always on time."

"Does she have any boyfriends or a fiancé?"

"Uh, she has a boyfriend who I don't think is good for her. She deserves better, but that's my opinion."

"What is this boyfriend's name, in case we have to check him?"

"I wish someone would check him. His name is Bruce Blair, and he lives in Roseville. His step-father is a cop from what I hear."

I felt a chill. "You don't know the cop's name, by chance?"

"I don't remember. It was some president's name, I think."

"Lincoln?"

"Yes, I think that was it. Abe Lincoln."

"Well, thank you for your time, Babs, I'll check back and talk to Melody later." I hung up and was amazed at how deep this was getting.

I would need to set up a timeline board to keep track of all the goings on. I went to my ample closet and pulled out the self-standing dry erase board I had been saving for just this occasion. I started writing all the characters' names and drawing lines to connect them and events. I taped a picture of Noreen in the center to keep my focus and stood back to examine the thing. The whole thing looked cock-eyed to me but made a bit more sense than trying to keep it all in my head.

The door opened, and Trapper popped his head in. "Ah, the crime board. Helps you stay organized, doesn't it?" He grinned.

He sat in the client's chair and put his feet up on my desk. I gave him a dirty look and took one foot down.

"So what's going on, and how is Bruce Blair hooked into it?" he said looking at my board.

Dominatrix Murders

I asked, "Do you know Bruce Blair?"

"Yep, a little con man who has crossed my path a few times. Is he really related to Lincoln?" Looking at my lines.

"Yeah, Lincoln's step-son."

"Wow, that's interesting. When we nabbed him he used his real father's info, never mentioned Lincoln. Hmm, Lincoln and Bruce both turn up in this case. Interesting. So what have you found out so far?"

I filled him in on all the details from the last time I saw him, and he just sat bobbling his head.

I finished and then asked him if he ever ran the plate from the car in the surveillance videos at the storage. He said he hadn't because he assumed they were from Lincoln. I asked if he could and took out the paper I had the plate number written on. He took my desk phone, called his precinct, and talked to someone in the system. He waited while they ran them and then he hung up.

He looked at me, smiled, and said, "The plates are registered to Bruce Blair. Now isn't that sweet?"

"OK, we now know Brucie is definitely involved with this. He's boyfriend to Melody, and she was working for Noreen," I said as I drew more lines on my board. "I think it's getting narrowed down. Melody and Bruce, or just Bruce, conspire to blackmail Noreen's clients using her name and then probably Noreen finds out, so they, or he, kills her. They, or he, keep blackmailing the clients, and then step-daddy Lincoln finds out step-boy is involved in the murder, takes over the case and tries to cover up. I wonder if he's getting a cut of the money, too."

"Lots of lines crossing over each other, but it's coming together," Trapper said as I stepped back to look at the mess.

"But if Lincoln is going around trying to find the list, how did they know who to blackmail? If Melody worked there long enough to recognize a few clients, they could start with that. But why would they need the list? Is Lincoln trying to protect someone he knows on that list before it gets out? Way too many questions and not enough answers."

"Welcome to the wonderful world of detecting. You never get answers right off, or they wouldn't need us." Trapper smiled.

"OK, this case isn't in your jurisdiction so you can't pull Bruce in, and I don't dare go to Lincoln to ask him to pull him in. So I got to skate around the whole thing on thin ice, especially if Bruce is living with Lincoln. I wonder where Melody goes during the day when she says she is going to work. Maybe

Dominatrix Murders

I need to go check out Noreen's office again. Care to join me?"

"What the hell, I'm not chasing crime in my town." He laughed. "May as well go invade someone else's town."

We headed out in our own cars, in case Trapper got a call to duty, and drove over to Noreen's office. I parked across the street, and Trapper pulled in behind me. We walked up to the office and were surprised to find it open. We walked in and found a smallish blond girl behind the desk. She smiled and welcomed us. I looked around and saw that it was a lot cleaner than the last time I was in there. I reached in my pocket and turned on the record button on my Palm just in case. I walked up to the desk and asked to see Mistress Black. The girl smiled and said Mistress Black was out of town for a week, but she could schedule an appointment if we liked. I asked her name. She said Melody and held out two three-by-five cards for us. She said to put our names and information and a little detail of the domination we desired.

I put the cards back on the table and asked, "Where might Mistress Black be at?"

"Oh, I'm not at liberty to say. It's confidential." She smiled.

I looked at Trapper and asked if he knew anyone in fraud or vice in Roseville. He said he did. I

166

looked at Melody and said, "Melody, Noreen is dead, but I'm sure you know that. I'm a private investigator, this gentleman is a police lieutenant, and we find it a bit odd that you didn't know your employer is deceased. You are either naïve, stupid, or you killed Noreen. Which is it?"

She had a panicked look on her face. "I didn't want to do this, but he said I'd die if I didn't keep up with the con."

"Who, Melody? Who warned you?" Trapper asked.

"My boyfriend, Bruce Blair. He said we should continue taking new clients to blackmail them since we didn't have Noreen's list." She started to tear up. "I said it was too risky, too soon after her death."

"Melody, who killed Noreen?" I asked.

She gave me a pained look and said, "I don't know. I came here to work the other day and Bruce's stepfather was here. He told me what happened to Noreen, and I went to Bruce and told him. Bruce was already blackmailing a couple of clients, and he didn't want to lose the con. I had a key to the office so we got in and cleaned it up, figuring the cops were done with it, so we could keep taking clients."

Dominatrix Murders

I took Trapper aside and said, "We can keep this away from Lincoln if you can get your vice friends to take this. It's fraud and blackmail, but nothing towards Lincoln's case of murder."

Trapper agreed, stepped out the front door, got on his cell phone, and made a few calls.

"Melody, how long did you think you could get away with this?" I asked her.

"I didn't think we could, but Bruce insisted we do it. I'm honestly afraid of him. He's nuts. I wish I never met him."

"Melody, we are having vice come in and arrest you. It will hopefully keep you safe for now and away from Lincoln who may be involved in ways I don't want to say right now. You will have to cooperate with the officers and let them know everything you know. Understand?" She nodded her head and started crying harder. I felt so sorry for her.

*

Chapter Twenty-three

Trapper came back in and said he had a friend on his way. He told his friend to keep it on the quiet and not let Lincoln in on it. His friend was not a fan of Lincoln and agreed. About ten minutes later an unmarked car and a patrol car pulled up. Trapper's friend entered, and I was introduced to Detective Sergeant Mike Gregory. We shook hands, and I filled him in on what was going on, all the way back to Noreen's death, which he knew about. Trapper explained that we needed to keep Melody out of Lincoln's hands. This had nothing to do directly with the murder, just an after effect of it. Gregory agreed and liked the premise of our plot.

Gregory went to Melody and read her the Miranda rights, explaining it to her. She was looking so wretched, I hated doing this to her, but it was for the best. Gregory sat and asked her a number of questions then called for a warrant on Blair. That ought to piss off Lincoln. They took Melody into custody, and I said to Trapper that I felt sorry for the girl, being dragged into this.

"Jim, you're going to have to toughen up a bit. First, she may be innocent, but after you get involved in a number of cases like this, you'll find that she was probably just as cooperative as Blair was in the crime. She's a big girl and knew what she was getting into."

Gregory came over. "Trapper, are things so slow in Clinton Township, you got to come to my turf and stir up trouble?"

"Don't look at me. I'm just an observer. Blame Richards here. It's his case. So far I'm getting sick of Roseville." He grinned.

"Well, this is going to piss off Lincoln one way or another. I look forward to booking that asshole kid of his. I hope Lincoln tries to start something with me. I've wanted to clean his clock for years. You guys going to lock up here?" he asked and then left after we said we'd take care of it.

"Jim, you are starting to get the swing of this business. Welcome to my world," Trapper offered.

Trapper headed back to his boundaries, and I went back to my office. I wondered what Buck was up to. I hadn't heard from him all day. I went in and called Benson's office and after he came on I explained about the incident at Noreen's office. His case with Weston was closed since I found the mystery woman, so there was no trial to go to. I asked if he ever did pro-bono work, and he said on rare occasions. I told him about Melody and her involvement in the con job Bruce was pulling. I said she was most likely guilty but I'd like to see the court go easy on her, if possible. Benson said he liked my compassion and would look into the case for me.

We finished and hung up. Then I got Frank Ropiello's number and called him. I reminded him who I was and told him about catching Bruce Blair as his possible blackmailer. I asked if he could identify the person who took the money. I assumed it was Bruce. He said he could, so I gave him the number off the business card Gregory gave me. I told him to call and explain what I told him and see if they could get him in a line-up. He thanked me and hung up.

I had done my good deeds for the day and was wondering how Penny was doing. I decided to close up and go home, so I headed out and drove over to Jefferson and into the drive. Penny said they had a child psychologist on her show that day so I couldn't see any surprises that Penny might throw at me. I was wrong. I got into the house and saw a child, about two years old staring at me from a crib in the middle of the family room. I just stood there hoping it would go away, but it was still watching me. Penny came into the room and said in a happy voice, welcome home, daddy.

"OK, did I miss something? Was I gone for a few years, and now I'm a father?"

Dominatrix Murders

Penny giggled, picked up the baby and brought it to me. I recoiled in fear. Penny said to stop that and act like a father.

I took the kid and said, "What do I do now, and where did this thing come from?"

"I kidnapped it from a playground," she said.

I looked at her as if she was crazy. "What did you say?"

"Oh, grow up. I'm babysitting for one of the girls on my staff, Liz Davis. She needed a babysitter, and I thought it would be a great idea. Liz lives out this way in Harrison Township and dropped the baby off."

I handed the kid back to her and said, "I hope the two of you are very happy together."

"If you ever want to have sex with me again, you will play daddy for a couple of hours, at least till Liz comes to get the baby."

I hemmed a bit and then said I would. She handed the baby back to me and said she had to go make us food for dinner. I went to the couch and yelled to Penny, "What is it? Boy or girl?"

Penny yelled back, "Her name is Diana. She's my god-child."

"Ah, I see. I guess. Where is the mother?"

"She's at a Lamaze class for her second child. Her partner and she are going natural childbirth."

"Her partner? As in husband or life partner?"

"Life partner, yes, Liz is gay."

I looked at the child and said, "Boy, I hope you're going to be strong. You're going to need it."

The baby goo'd and flashed her long eyelashes at me. I thought she was kind of cute. I bounced her on my knee, and she started laughing and giggling aloud. Penny peeked in and saw what I was doing, came over and kissed me on my bald head, then went back into the kitchen.

We ate dinner of tacos, and baby had something out of a jar, something that didn't look very appetizing. After dinner I took the baby, went to the family room and put her on the couch next to me. She was waving her arms around and hitting my arm.

"Yep, she's a female, already beating on a man," I kidded.

Penny came out and sat on the other side of her. The baby crawled over and tried to latch on to one of Penny's breasts. I said, "Hey, that's mine. You get the bottle while you're here." I picked up her bottle and pulled her to me, laying her on her back, then inserted the nipple into her mouth. Penny sat and watched me with the child. She wished she was able to have children and wondered if we were too old to adopt. She knew at 60 we would be too old to take care of a child, and with her show and my out playing detective, it wouldn't be fair to the baby. So she enjoyed the moment.

"I went through all this with my son. I've been there. Not that I want to do it again. I can't change diapers, I have a low threshold for odors, I gag big time," I warned. Penny laughed and said she'd take care of that end.

We played with the child for a few more hours and then the doorbell rang. It was Liz. She came into the family room. I was on the ground with the baby on my belly, bouncing her.

Penny said, "Now you see what I go through every night." She laughed and came to rescue the child. Liz thanked Penny and me for watching Diana. I said, no problem, just don't let it happen again. Penny whacked me on the arm, and Liz laughed.

"I've heard all about you, Jim, Penny tells us all kinds of gory tales. Especially the ones with handcuffs." She smiled.

"Someone is in trouble tonight," I mumbled.

Liz thanked us again and went off after I put the crib in her car. I wondered where her partner was. Penny said she worked late nights and had to be back to her job. We went back into the house, and I said that we needed to discuss what tales she's been telling at work, but later. We plopped down on the couch, and I told her about the councilman, the Dom pretending to be Elvira and then about Melody and her part in the thing along with bad boy Bruce and that I got Benson to try and help her. Penny kissed me on the cheek and said I was an old softy.

We watched TV for a while, drinking our beer, eating potato chips and smooching at every commercial. Life was good.

*

Chapter Twenty-four

Next morning Penny had left and I was just getting ready to go out the door to my office when the phone rang. It was Detective Gregory.

"Richards, we brought in Blair this morning. I thought you might want to be in on the interrogation and line-up." I said I would like that, might hear something to help my case. He said they would have him in around 9:15, so be there. I hung up and drove over to Roseville precinct, feeling a little apprehensive about Lincoln being there. Maybe I should have called Trapper. No, I couldn't depend on Trapper to always watch my back. I'd have to face him myself.

I got there and was directed to where they had the line-up. Gregory saw me and said to follow him. We went into the observation room, and I saw Frank Ropiello. He acknowledged me, and then Gregory explained what we were going to do. There was another man in the room in a fancy suit. I figured he was a lawyer. Gregory called through a microphone to bring the men in. Just as they were coming in, the observation room door opened and in walked Lincoln. He had no expression when he saw me, just went to the other side of the room. Gregory gave him a dirty look, like don't screw around with my witness, as he moved over between Lincoln and Ropiello to where Ropiello couldn't see Lincoln. The men were all lined up, and the lights were brought up on them. Ropiello just stood staring as he went from face to face.

"Take your time, Councilman Ropiello. Do you see the man who was threatening you with blackmail and taking money from you?" Gregory asked.

Ropiello looked hard and finally said it was number three, which happened to be Blair. "That man came to my office twice to take money from me and warn me not to talk or my unusual

176

predilections would be all over the papers. I've already confessed to my wife about it. I was only there a couple of times, so I'm ready to be a witness."

Gregory thanked Ropiello and told him they'd talk to him about what needed to be done, maybe they could just take his statement, and he might not have to testify as a protected witness. Ropiello thanked him and left, followed by Lincoln. I looked at Gregory and went out to see where Lincoln was going. He went the opposite way from Ropiello and down a hall. Gregory followed me out and said, "Now to roast the little dickhead."

We went to a different side of the building, and Gregory pointed to a door saying that was where I should go. I went in and found Lincoln sitting quietly in a chair. Leaning up against the back wall was the same guy in the suit. He smiled at me and introduced himself at an assistant DA.

Lincoln didn't look at me, but said, "I hear you're responsible for Bruce being brought in."

"I caught Melody in her little scam. Blair was a casualty of that. He's a big boy and knew what he was doing was illegal. From what I hear she feared for her life from Blair if she didn't go along with the scam. Not a good boy in there."

"I didn't raise him. That son of a bitch convict father of his screwed him over good. I can't change

177

him now." He went silent, and I had nothing more to say.

If Lincoln didn't care so much for step-boy, why was he here? Maybe to see if Blair would rat him out. I watched as Blair squirmed in his chair until Gregory came in. He gave Gregory a dirty look as the big man sat across from him. Gregory stared, Blair looked uncomfortable, then Gregory spoke.

"Bruce, this is the third time I've had a talk with you. Just can't stay out of trouble, can you? Just get yourself in deeper don't you?" he started.

Blair gave him a stupid expression and kept watching the door as if he were expecting Lincoln to come to his rescue.

"Bruce, we definitely got you for blackmailing a city official. You were picked out of the line-up as the blackmailer. We are going to be adding a murder charge to that, too. How's that?"

Bruce went up to being alert now. "I had nothing to do with any murder! I didn't kill the bitch. I don't know who did!" he whined.

"Well, Bruce, let's see, you were blackmailing Noreen Black's clients, and I'll bet she found out, so you had to silence her. Isn't that the way it went down?"

"No! Melody was supplying me with names of people she recognized coming into the office, and she told me what to do for getting the money out of them. Maybe Melody killed Black. I didn't!"

"Did Melody have access to Black's client list?"

"Hell, no. Black didn't share that list with anyone. We don't even know where she hid it. We looked after work hours. She didn't have it in her office. I even broke into her house one afternoon to see if I could find it. Melody also heard Black mention she had a storage unit. I went there and found some videos and stuff that I thought would help us. They didn't do us any good, though."

Now I knew who the mystery intruder was at Weston's house and at the storage unit.

He continued, "So Melody said we would just work on the clients she knew. Before long we'd have a good base built up."

I was starting to wonder if Trapper was right about feeling sorry for people. If Bruce was too stupid to lie, maybe Melody wasn't all that innocent. I had better have a talk with Benson to get his take.

"When did you start blackmailing clients?"

"Just after Melody started working there. We thought it would be a quick buck. About two weeks later, Black was dead. I didn't have anything to do with it. I swear!"

"Did you tell those people you were blackmailing that Black was involved in the scam?"

"We didn't say she was. I guess people just assumed she was behind it."

"Didn't you even think someone might have wanted her dead rather than being blackmailed and exposed?"

"No, we didn't think that."

"You know all the people you were scamming. I want a list of their names. Just maybe we can find someone in that list that might have killed Black. That would get you off the hook for the actual deed, wouldn't it?"

"Yeah, I can do that! I'll give you what you want."

"Tell me, Bruce, it was your idea to blackmail the clients, wasn't it?"

"Hell, no! Melody met me one night after she got off work and told me how we could make a lot of money if we played our cards right. I went along, I thought it would work. We hadn't counted on Black getting iced," he lamented.

"Where were you the night she was iced?"

"I was at a bachelor party for a buddy, I got plenty of witnesses. I'll give you plenty of names." He smirked.

"OK, Bruce, we got you for blackmail and fraud, you better hope we don't take you down for murder," Gregory said as he stood then went out.

Lincoln was quiet then stood. He looked at me but said nothing and went out. I could swear I saw a little sadness in his eyes. I didn't want to start feeling sorry for him now. Gregory popped his head in the door and asked if I wanted to go watch him question Melody. I did. We went to a different room. I was followed by the suit, and I stood looking at Melody sitting quietly at the table. Lincoln walked in and stood at the back of the room, didn't say a word.

Gregory walked in and sat, opening up a folder. "Melody, I've talked to Bruce, and he had some interesting things to say."

I could see her eyes perk up. Gregory was going to play her against Bruce.

"Bruce forced me to do the blackmail. He threatened me if I didn't help, he would hurt me," she whined.

"Well, Melody, Bruce said it was your idea to do the blackmailing. Is he lying?"

"Of course he's lying. Look at his record. He's a con man from way back."

"Where did you two meet, when you first got together?"

"I met him at a party one of my girlfriends was throwing. I didn't know anything about him at the time, but he was a good talker. We started seeing each other after that."

"How long before you started working for Noreen Weston?"

"About two months."

"Enough time to realize he was a trouble maker. Did you take into account his criminal past when you decided to start blackmailing people?"

"I knew he had a checkered past, but he came up with the idea to do the scam after I told him about my job. I didn't like it, but he kept at me about how much money we could make. Then he started threatening me if I didn't help."

"Why didn't you just leave him?"

"He wouldn't let me go. He'd just find me. I feared him."

"Did Bruce do the killing of Noreen or was that your doing."

She looked shocked and cried, "I didn't have anything to do with her murder! Bruce didn't either. He was too stupid to do something on his own." That statement made me think.

"Then who did it, Melody?"

"I have no idea. I was with girlfriends that night while Bruce was at a bachelor party. I can prove it."

"If you want to cover your ass, Melody, I'd recommend you give us a list of the people you blackmailed. We may be able to sort out a killer in the bunch. How many people did you scam?"

"We had about six people involved. I'll give you a list if it will help."

"Didn't you think maybe one of the people who feared they would be exposed might want to kill the person they thought was blackmailing them?"

She was quiet for a bit then softly said, "No."

"Well, even if you didn't do the kill, you are just as responsible for her death, so I'd think about that. Maybe you can get some retribution by helping us catch the real killer." He tossed her a pad and pencil and told her to start writing names and anything she knew about the people they blackmailed. She started writing on the pad, and I started thinking about calling Benson and talking to him about this.

*

Chapter Twenty-five

Lincoln was the first to leave the room, followed by the suit. I stood for a minute till Gregory walked in.

"Well, what do you think?" he asked.

"Well, I've talked to a number of people who all led me around in circles in the last couple days. No one wants to say anything about the fetishes of others. I can understand that. I dress up in women's clothes, and I don't want people to know." I grinned.

"Don't fuck with me. I'm just getting to like you. I can slip you a copy of the blackmail list. I'm not supposed to, but I think I can just set it somewhere that you can find it," he said. "I don't want this buried in Lincoln's case files and not go anywhere. You can shake the trees and see what monkeys fall out."

"Is that a discriminatory remark against monkeys?" I joked.

"I may be black and beautiful, but a racist I'm not." Gregory laughed.

"So what are you going to do now with blondie and the boob?" I asked.

"We've definitely got them for blackmail and fraud. It should stick. They confessed in front of the assistant DA. We have their statements, and they gave up the clients being blackmailed so we can pursue the murder aspect. Or I should say, Lincoln will pursue. At least, I hope he does. It's his case. Otherwise, I'm done with this till their trial."

I shook his hand and thanked him for letting me in on the interrogations. He said if it wasn't for my snooping, they wouldn't have gotten this far. An officer came up and handed Gregory a sheet of paper. He looked at it and set it on a desk.

"Now don't you pick up that paper. It's only for official people to see." He grinned then walked away. I looked around and picked up the paper, stuffed it in my pocket and walked out.

I sat in my car and looked at the paper. I was shocked to see the quality of people who had fetishes that they wanted to play out. I drove to my office, and on the way called Trapper.

"What do you want now?" he yelled. I laughed and told him I had the official list of perverts in and around Macomb County. He choked and said how long before I was in my office. I said about fifteen minutes. He said he'd meet me. I drove on and then into my parking lot. I saw Trapper's car. He must have used his flashers and siren. I came into my lobby and found him sitting, talking to a great looking blond. He saw me and said he had to go but gave her his card in case she ever needed a cop. I just rolled my eyes and opened my office. I turned back to the lobby as he came in and smiled at the blond. She waved her fingers at me, and I closed the door.

"You dog, it's a good thing you're not married. Did you get her number?" I asked.

"Oh, yeah, I got her number the minute I saw her. She's a hooker," he said.

I stood looking at him. "What? A hooker? What's she doing in my lobby?"

"Jim, didn't you know that there is a travel agency upstairs that hires hookers to go on cruises for lonely men?"

I was stunned. "No, I didn't know that. How do they get away with it?"

"Well, it's out of the country, so we can't do much about it. Once they're out in international waters they can do what they want, sex-wise, and collect money which is transferred from the ship to an off shore account. All sort of legal." He grinned.

"Damn, my dreams are shattered," I said.

"Well, at least you can enjoy the parade through your lobby." He laughed.

"Yeah, true. OK, I have a list of people blackmailed by the bad news lovers. If you can look it over, maybe we can decide who the really bad person in this scenario is," I offered.

He took the paper I was holding out and looked at it for a long while. He whistled and said, "This is hot. Does Lincoln have this yet?"

"I'm sure he does by now unless Gregory is wasting time moving it around the system," I said.

"Well, there are three big name politicians here, one owner of a large chain of appliance stores and two local TV celebrities, news and weather. That would make for a great breaking news story." He was grinning from ear to ear.

I said I had read the list. "But who do you think may have killed Noreen?"

Dominatrix Murders

"Not a single person on this list, but then again, I have seen cases where a priest committed murder."

I just stared at him. He continued, "OK, I exaggerated, but the point is these people have a lot more to lose if they commit murder than they would for just being spanked."

"I'd say the politicians would be my first choice for murderers. They're all cut-throats," I said.

"You don't like lawyers and politicians, we get that. But this list has no one on here that sends my radar into overdrive. Sorry, maybe one of them did do it, but I can't tell," he offered.

"OK, out of the list, let's prioritize top to bottom who may be the most likely suspects," I said. "Oh, and we can rule out Ropiello. He's come forward and done his duty to fight crime, and he's a wuss from my contact with him."

"Well, the one to lose the most would be the judge, then the guy who owns the stores—bad publicity makes bad sales—then the city planner, although no one pays any attention to them. The TV people wouldn't ruin their careers by killing someone, so they're last," he offered.

"The TV people are both from Penny's station. I'll have to ask her about them." I sat looking at the list.

"You know it could be someone not even on this list." I sighed. "Someone who Noreen had as a customer but who might have had a problem with her or she might have wanted more from him. Weston did say she was going to hit people up for more money. I wish we knew where her list was."

"We have to figure Lincoln in on this, too. How is he connected to any of these people, or was he a customer, too, and afraid of exposure?" Trapper wondered.

"If I were Eve Dallas, I'd run this by the computer for probabilities." Trapper looked at me funny. "Sorry, you had to be there," I said.

"Sometimes I wonder about you." He smirked. "Well, you just have to go bother people and see who doesn't like it the most. Just don't get yourself hacked up and decapitated."

"That's another thing, the way Noreen was killed. Hacked by what they think was a machete. Who carries a machete around with them nowadays?" I asked.

"I saw the appliance guy hacking prices on one of his TV ads. He used a machete," Trapper said.

"Yeah, I remember that one, too. I think I'm safe in starting with him." I grinned. "Want to go with me?"

Dominatrix Murders

"Nah, I hate his commercials, so I don't really want to meet the guy. Besides, my Captain is starting to wonder why my work log is so lopsided with others doing all the work. I got to put in some effort to look busy. I'll pass." He smiled and got up, saluted me and headed out the door.

I sat for a bit then looked up the corporate headquarters for Doan Appliances and found the address was in Chesterfield Township, Buck's backyard. I was beginning to wonder what happened to Buck. He hadn't called in for over a day and a half or even popped in for a visit. I was worrying a bit. I picked up my phone to call just as the door opened and Buck strolled in.

"Damn, I was just calling you. I was wondering what happened to you," I said. "You've been gone for over a day."

"I got lucky. Remember that fox in the hallway the other day?" I nodded. He continued, "Well, she followed me out of the building when I left, and we started talking by my car. She was asking me about myself, and then we started talking about cars, and I told her about my classic cars, and she said she wanted to see mine. So she followed me to my place, and I showed her. She stayed till this morning. What a woman."

"Buck, she's a hooker," I said quietly.

He looked at me and then smiled. "She never charged me, so she couldn't have been a hooker."

"Well, Trapper told me the travel agency upstairs is a front for a floating cat house. They offer cruises to lonely men with all these gorgeous women, the ones who come through here. That fox was probably one, and I would watch your cars so they don't disappear," I warned.

He stood and said he had to go take care of something then went out the door quickly. I had to suppress a laugh. I hoped she didn't have robbery on her mind.

*

Chapter Twenty-six

I drove up Gratiot towards Chesterfield Township and, after checking my Palm map program, I found Doan Appliance's headquarters and went into the parking lot. I went in the building and stopped at the desk in the lobby. The girl asked me my purpose for being there, and I said I wanted to see Mr. Doan. She asked if I had an appointment. I said no, but if she would call Mr. Doan and mention the name Noreen Black, I was sure he'd want to see me. She got on the phone and called, stating my request, then hung up. She said Mr. Doan would be with me shortly.

I hardly turned to sit down when a skinny young man came out from a side door and asked my name. I told him. He said to follow him, and we went through a long series of hallways. The young man was talking into a device sticking out of his ear. I heard him mention my name, and then we came to a big double walnut door and went in.

Doan was sitting behind a huge, fancy desk made of expensive looking wood trimmed with shiny metal. Behind him the entire wall was one gigantic window looking out on a well-managed flower garden and woods. He was sitting back in his chair and had a look of arrogance on his face.

"Mr. Richards, sit, please." I did. He continued, "I instructed my assistant here to call the police in five minutes unless I stop him. I will not tolerate any more blackmail from your people. This will cease now, and I will take my medicine for my mistakes, but you will be in prison." He smiled like he had won a round.

"Mr. Doan, the people involved in your blackmail are already in jail. I saw to that yesterday. I'm not here to blackmail you. I'm a private investigator hired by Noreen Black's husband to find her killer. You can call off your poodle now," I said, looking at the skinny young assistant.

Bob Moats

Doan stopped smiling, was quiet for a moment, then nodded to the assistant and told him to leave us alone. He did.

"Mr. Doan, I'm here to ask you a few questions, that's all. I don't care one way or another what you do in your private time. I'm looking for a murderer. You wouldn't happen to be that murderer, would you?"

He studied me for a bit then smiled. "You're direct, Mr. Richards, but no, I'm not the murderer. I, of course, wouldn't admit it even if I was.

Doan wasn't at all like the character he portrayed in his commercials, that annoying, loud mouthed buffoon doing his best to draw you into his stores with promises of cheap prices. He was cool and calm, very calculating in his demeanor.

"I didn't expect you to confess, Mr. Doan, but where were you on the night Ms. Black was murdered?" I asked.

"Since you are not an actual police officer, I really don't have to answer your questions, now do I?" His smile widened, and I could see he had a nice set of teeth, probably paid for by many washer sales.

"Well, Mr. Doan, you don't have to, but if I can narrow down the list of suspects quickly, then you don't have to go through the pain of having to talk

193

to the real police and possibly get your name in the papers. So you can go that route or help me." I gave him my big smile back.

His eyes narrowed, and his smile wavered. "All right, Mr. Richards, I was with my wife at a party thrown by the Mayor of Warren to celebrate business owners in his city. My store there does the best over all the other stores. I was with about a hundred other business owners, and I even gave a little speech about the business climate in Warren. Does that answer your question?"

"Quite well enough. I'll cross you off my list. Hated to bother you, but it's a messy business. Oh, one more thing, whatever happened to that machete you used in one of your commercials to hack at prices?" I asked.

His face totally dropped, and his eyes glazed, then he said calmly, "I don't know, it was a prop from the commercial filmers. They probably have it."

"Strange thing, it was believed a machete was used to kill Noreen. Did you hear about that?" I pushed.

"No, I heard she was butchered, but not how it was committed. Are you done, Mr. Richards?" he said quietly.

"For now, Mr. Doan. Oh, and a very big, ugly police detective by the name of Lincoln, as in honest Abe, probably will be stopping by to talk, too. Give him my regards." I stood and said, "I think I can find my way out." I left him looking annoyed.

I didn't like the man. He was cocky and arrogant. I actually liked his TV persona better. But I saw a bit of something in his eyes when I mentioned the machete. Maybe nothing, but I was going to move him up the list. I got to the lobby and saw his assistant.

"Excuse me. I really like the Doan Appliance commercials. Who creates those?" I asked.

He smiled and said, "My cousin Harvey. He has a company that does the commercials. It's Marco Productions."

I thanked him and said they were great. I lied. He had one of those nametags on. It said Ken Reed. I took note, went to my car and drove out.

I went by Buck's place since it was just up the road and pulled in the long drive. I remembered the last time I was there, back when we were trying to hide Penny from the killers of the cheerleaders. It took me back seeing the place. I saw a truck in front of Buck's van and pulled up next to it. The signage on the truck door said "Mavis Security and Alarms." I had to laugh. Buck saw me as he stood in

195

front of his garage and came over as I got out of my car.

"What's happening, Buck?" I knew, but asked.

"I'm protecting my investment. I got back here after I talked to you and saw a car sitting across the street looking at my property. They took off as I pulled up and got out to go see what the hell they were doing. You may have been right about that hooker, Jimmy." He looked crushed, like she used him.

"Don't take it personal, Buck. They do this crap every day to people just like you. Good thing you're preparing for it."

He smiled and handed me a piece of paper. It had a license plate number on it. "I guess hanging around a P.I. must be rubbing off on me. I got his plates." He looked happy now.

"I'll give this to Trapper and see what comes up. Just may be part of a car theft ring. Better yet, you call him and explain what is going on and ask. It might start good relations with the two of you."

He didn't say anything, but then smiled and said he'd do just that.

The alarm installer called to Buck with a question and he went off to answer it. I stood looking at the yard where we had our party with the motorcycle club the night before Penny was kidnapped. Buck came back to me, and I told him about Doan and what I found out. I said I was going to check out his commercial makers and check a detail that might help my case. Buck said he'd join up with me later and went back to the installer.

I sat in my car and looked up the address for Marco Productions in the phone book I keep in the car. I drove out, headed to Sterling Heights, and found the building that housed Marco. I pulled in and went up to the entrance but found a note saying to use the side door. I went around to where the arrow led me and into the building. I came into a big hangar- like room where they were filming a commercial for some awning company. One man spotted me and came over.

"May I help you?" he asked.

"Yes, is Harvey in?" I replied.

"I'm Harvey. What can I do for you?"

"I got your name from your cousin Ken Reed. He said you film the Doan commercials."

"Yes, we do, our biggest account."

"Can we talk somewhere private?" I asked.

He led me to a small conference room and asked me to sit.

"I'm a private investigator, and I'm checking on a few things in regard to a case I'm working on. I was wondering if you remember the commercial you created with Doan hacking prices with a machete."

"Oh, yeah, Doan loved that one. I think he got a kick out of swinging the thing. He was hacking at anything that wasn't moving. I was a little worried he might hurt someone with it. The damn thing was sharp."

"Do you still have that prop?"

"As a matter of fact, we don't. When the commercial was finished, Doan wanted to keep the thing. Hey, after he spent thousands of dollars on the commercial, he could keep anything he wanted. So Doan has the machete."

*

Chapter Twenty-seven

I said that was all I needed to know and thanked him for his time. He led me to the locked front door that led to my car. I sat in my car for a bit and then chuckled to myself. I pictured Doan swinging that machete around hacking at prices flying at him and screaming, "I'm slashing high prices so you can save big at Doan Appliances!" Guess it wasn't the only thing he was slashing. I needed to find the machete, but where would it be? I was sure he would have disposed of it, so it could be in any number of garbage dumps or buried in a backyard. I thought about his fancy flower garden out back of his building and wondered if maybe he buried it there. I knew he had a thing for the weapon. Maybe he put it someplace nearby.

I was really hungry, so I stopped at the nearest Subway I could find and had lunch. I was mulling over my morning and wondering if I should go bother a judge about his involvement in the case. I thought about going to Penny's studio and questioning the news people on the list, might just stir up some talk about the murder, but I didn't really think they did it. I was really liking Doan for the killings. I took my time eating, just relaxing, then I finally finished my lunch, got back out to my car and drove to my office. I was surprised to see two patrol cars, one unmarked, sitting in my parking lot. I saw Trapper off to the side standing next to his car. He waved at me. I went over.

"What's going on?" I asked.

"Well, Buck called me and told me about his run in with the hooker. I had to laugh to myself, I didn't want to offend him. The plate numbers he gave me came up to a prior felon, Joe Michaels, a car thief, known to live in my town. I took a couple of men with me and we found a chop shop in his double sized garage. After threats of the rubber hose, Joe finally told me that he got his info for available cars to steal from a couple of girls who worked out of this office. So I talked to the Fraser police, and we conducted a little raid. Looks like you may not have your parade of babes anymore." He grinned.

I was crushed. I enjoyed watching the girls go by. I looked at him and said, "I'm hearing about this rubber hose from you and Lawson. What the hell is it?"

He grinned. "It's just the way we threaten a suspect with all kinds of torture and spending life behind bars. All talk, but it works."

"Ah, I see," I said as the Fraser police were escorting three beauties and one male to the waiting cars. Trapper said they'd be out by tomorrow, there was lots of money behind this operation. They'll just go set up somewhere else.

About a half hour later the Fraser cops were gone, and Trapper and I sat in my office as I filled him in on my visit with Doan.

"I knew he was a little prick from his commercials," Trapper said.

"Yep, and I would love to know where the machete ended up," I offered. "Unfortunately, there are a million places he could have disposed of it, any number of box crushers in his stores, or just a drop in some garbage can alongside the road. It could even be in the St. Clair River by now. I wouldn't know where to start, but I had one odd thought about his botanical garden out back of his headquarters. Might be buried out there."

"Well, Lincoln has the power to do a search for the weapon, with a warrant, if he was doing his job. Maybe you should go talk with him. If he knows you know, it may force him to do something about it," Trapper offered.

"After the way he was in the interrogation, I can believe he would do that. I can't figure his place in this whole thing. Bruce and Melody never said anything about him and the blackmail. So far he hasn't done anything out of the ordinary to look criminal. I'm thinking he thought his step-son was involved in the murders and was trying to find out, or to cover his ass, but that would be bad for Lincoln if he was found out. I can't really say he was going to shoot that store clerk. He may just like holding on to his weapon." I sat back and wondered.

"Well, he's not one of the police department's finest, but he is the man on the case. May need to bring him up to speed," Trapper said. "Let's go have a little talk with him."

I looked at Trapper like he had offered to go into combat with me. "You want to go right now?" I asked.

"Sure, I did my duty today, broke up a chop shop, that should keep my captain happy for a day or two." He grinned. "Besides, you haven't annoyed Lincoln today, so we can rectify that situation."

We went to our own cars and headed to Roseville. We were taken to Lincoln's cubby hole. He grumbled, "What do you two want?"

I sat on the chair next to his desk. "Be nice. I have some info to share with you. If you are still on the Weston case."

He was silent, then, "What?"

I told him about visiting Doan in the course of my investigation and the connection I made with the machete commercial and the machete death of Noreen. I told him that the commercial company said Doan kept the machete and the mood he was in with said machete. Lincoln just sat listening.

"Not bad, it's usable," he said. Then he sat back in his chair and looked at Trapper then me. "I know I'm not liked very much. I am a bit abrasive, more than I should be. But I take my job seriously, sometimes too much. After twenty-five years on the force, I've seen too much to make my stomach turn." He looked at Trapper, who nodded back knowingly. "I hope this pans out. I'd like to go out with one good bust under my belt. I'm retiring when this is over. You really think that Doan may have the guts to pull off a murder?"

"I have a gut feeling myself that he knows more than he is admitting. The machete connection is what makes me wonder," I answered.

"I'll need to go talk to this commercial maker to get an official position on it. I'll get back to you if I get a warrant, but where the fuck do I start to look for the weapon? He's got a huge empire to hide it in," Lincoln said.

"I got the feeling he wouldn't get rid of it, but I could be wrong. I wish I could give you an answer," I said.

"You're a pretty snoopy guy. Maybe you could snoop around and find something that might help," he said slyly.

"I could do that." I paused, then asked, "Since we're playing nice here, I need to know a couple things. Can we talk honestly?"

He sat forward again, and looked at Trapper then said, "Sit down, Trapper, get comfortable."

Trapper pulled up a chair from the side and sat. He had an idea of what I was going to do.

"Let's play nice, then," Lincoln said.

"OK, explain to me the Weston photo fuck-up."

"Just that, a fuck-up. The cop who started the case was handling it bad. His filing system was screwed up, and I got the wrong photos from him when they pulled him off the case. I read the files and went on my hunt without even meeting Weston, my first mistake. That barmaid couldn't I.D. him from the wrong photo so I assumed he was lying. No evidence from the motel, so more lying assumed. I will admit I fucked up on that whole mess." He went quiet again.

"Someone took a couple of shots at me and Marylou Martin outside the Midnight bar when I found her. What's your take on that?"

"Don't know, hadn't heard about it till now. Did anyone else know you were tracking her?"

"Just the lawyer and Trapper. Weston gave me his info from the jail, so I don't know if he talked to anyone else. I could have been watched and followed from going to Noreen's office." I paused, then, "Did Bruce have an interest in stopping Martin from talking, maybe to see Weston go to prison?"

"That kid is such a dip shit, he may have."

"I shot out the shooter's back car window. Did Bruce have a back window of his car missing?"

Lincoln's eyes narrowed. "Yeah, he said he was vandalized. I'll take care of that with him, if I have to. He'll face attempted murder charges. I don't condone anything he did. Step-son or not."

I hated to admit it, but I was sort of liking Lincoln about then.

*

Chapter Twenty-eight

"Well, if I find anything good to help get you a warrant, I think it would be good to go to Judge Mortimore. He's on the list of blackmailed suspects, too. Just to see what he does," I said.

For the first time since I'd known Lincoln, he cracked a smile. "Yeah, I like that too."

"How'd you find out who was on the blackmail list from Bruce and Melody?" Lincoln asked.

"I saw Gregory put it on a desk and I kind of snooped a look, just to help my case." I didn't tell him Gregory knew I had it or that I took it with me. What I told him was good enough.

"You are good at snooping aren't you?" He smiled again.

I stood and said, "Well, I'll let you do your thing and I'll go do mine." I added, "I'll keep you informed as to my progress."

Lincoln stood, too, said he would, also, and held his hand out. I shook it and felt like a barrier was broken. Trapper nodded to him, and we left.

"Well, that was a revelation," I said when we reached the parking lot. Trapper laughed and agreed.

"What are you going to do now?" Trapper asked.

"Well, Lincoln asked me to snoop. I just may do that. But I'll need good criminal help. I'm calling Buck."

Trapper laughed out loud, got into his car and headed out. I got on my cell phone, called Buck, and asked what he was up to. He said he was polishing his babies, and I asked if he wanted to go commit a misdemeanor. He said he'd love to, and I told him to meet me at my office.

About a half hour later Buck came in and sat. I filled him in on what happened after he called Trapper.

"Damn, the ladies won't be parading by anymore?" he lamented.

"Nope, they're all gone. Sorry, Buck, but at least your cars are safe now," I offered.

"So what kind of crime are we going to be committing?" he asked.

"When it's safe to go, we are going to be trespassing around a garden hunting for a machete."

He just stared and snickered. "We are going to be digging up a garden to find a big knife?"

"No digging." I got up, went to my ample closet and took out two metal detectors I'd had for years. I gave one to Buck, pulled up a chair next to him and showed him how they worked. I stood and showed him how to swing it and to listen for the sound of metal. I put a couple of metal items on the floor and showed the way they sound when detecting an object.

"These won't find dead bodies, will they?" he asked.

"Not unless they have metal in them."

"OK, this looks like fun. Can I borrow this to go to the park and hunt for treasure?" he asked.

"Sure, anytime you want. We need to wait till Doan is closed for the night and go when it's dark. I checked my moon phase program on my Palm, and there is a full moon tonight, luckily. Take it home with you and play with it in your yard, get used to it. I have extra batteries if needed." I showed him the pointed tool used to probe the ground for the metal objects and gave him a small trowel used to dig up the finds. I gave him the instruction book to look over and sent him home. I said I'd call him and we'd meet at his place and go from there. He went off.

It was almost 4 p.m., and I decided to go back home and see what Penny was up to. I forgot to ask her who was on her show that day so it would be a surprise when I got there. Lately, she was having themes at home, bringing her work home to bug me. I was dreading going back that night since I didn't know what to expect.

I drove up to the house. Nothing moved, and the door didn't open when got there. I went in and it was quiet, so I went to the back and saw Penny out in the yard with an artist easel painting on a small canvas.

I came out. She saw me, smiled and said, "Take your clothes off. I want to paint you nude."

"Hardly." I came up and saw she had painted a picture of the lake and the backyard. It wasn't half bad. "Not bad. It looks good. You had an artist on your show today?"

"Yes, sir, he's a convict who paints jailhouse portraits now." I looked at her and said I hoped she didn't invite him home. "No, sweetie, they wouldn't let him go out on his own. They had guards watching him." She reached down to the side of her easel and brought up a portrait of her. It was good. "The artist painted this while he was in the studio. Everyone loved it. He can paint one of these in less than 20 minutes."

Dominatrix Murders

"Why is he in jail?" I asked, sort of knowing.

"Art forgery, what else?" she said, as if it was funny, which it was.

"Ah, stands to reason. I'm going to be going back out tonight with Buck. We're going to trespass on Doan Appliance property."

"That's nice, sweetie. Don't get caught," she said matter-of-factly as she painted. Sometimes she amazed me. I said to enjoy her painting and went in the house to look for dark clothes to wear.

Around 9:30, after I told her about my day and my visit to Doan, she said she'd never buy from them again. We had dinner and watched a bit of TV. I said I was going to pick up Buck. She said to be careful and went back to painting a fruit bowl on the dining room table.

I called Buck, told him I was on my way, and asked if he understood the metal detector. He said he found 78 cents in his yard, and he definitely was going to be borrowing it again. I got to his house, we put the detectors in a duffel bag and headed off to Doan's offices. I parked in the lot next to Doan's, a warehouse for a furniture company, and we crossed over onto Doan's property.

"I hope he doesn't have some kind of security system out here," I said.

Bob Moats

We didn't hear any alarms, nor did any lights go on, so we made it to the side of the garden. I whispered to Buck to go to the other side and sweep back through the flowerbeds towards the middle where we would meet. If he found something, signal to me. He went around to the other side and started his search. The moon was just enough so we could see the ground, but not enough to make us very visible in our dark clothes.

I was finding a number of junk metal items, and nothing good was hitting. I was almost to the center of the garden, as was Buck, when I heard a car door slam. Buck heard it, too, and we ran to the back of the yard and into the trees and bushes. We watched as a figure came around the building, carrying something that looked like a grocery bag. The figure went to the side of the flower bed, pulled out a trowel from the bag, and started digging what looked like a deep hole. Then the figure put something into the hole and covered it. Smoothing the ground around it, the person went back to the side of the building, and we heard a car door slam again. A car started, and we could hear it drive away. We waited about five minutes and then ventured out. We went to the spot where the hole was dug. I swept the metal detector over until I hit something big. We carefully dug until we found the item. It was wrapped in newspaper. I put on the rubber gloves I brought, carefully opened one end and found it was what we hoped for, a machete blade sticking out of the partially unwrapped paper. Buck gave a quiet cheer. I re-wrapped the package and buried it back in the hole. I stuck a small stick into the ground to mark the spot, and we headed out quickly.

Back at Buck's, we celebrated with soft drinks since that was all Buck had, and I told him my plan to reveal the weapon to Lincoln. Buck asked how I knew the thing would be back there. I said I didn't, but it was some place to start. Although it wasn't back there when we started, we got lucky that Doan did decide to hide it back there.

I said I was going to head back home, and he could keep the detector till we needed it again. I drove back to the house and found Penny asleep on the couch. I gently woke her and just about carried her to the bedroom. I undressed her, tucked her in, then went out to the kitchen for a brew. I deserved it. We found the murder weapon and our killer. Now to let Lincoln have the glory. He deserved it, I felt. Besides, he would retire now and be out of everyone's hair.

*

Chapter Twenty-nine

The next morning I was awakened by Penny standing over the bed with a bed tray of breakfast. I sat up and asked why I deserved this, she should be the one getting breakfast in bed. She climbed in with me and said this was for both of us. We had our breakfast, feeding each other, then we went to take a shower together and toweled each other off. A good morning all around.

She was heading out the door when I stopped her and asked what new ventures would await me that evening. She laughed and said I had nothing to worry about. She had a program today about female problems. Nothing to do with me unless I got cramps once a month. I said I thankfully didn't and kissed her good-bye. I called Trapper and happily told him of our findings from last night and that I was going to see Lincoln today. He said that was good, now Lincoln could retire in peace. Then he wondered if they would be doing Doan's commercials from prison. I laughed and said I'd fill him in later on what happened today.

I drove over to Roseville, parked, and went into Lincoln's cubbyhole. He was doing some paper work and saw me coming.

"Any good news, Mr. Snoop?" he asked, fairly cheerful.

"Oh, you're going to love this." I told him about our adventures in the garden and the mysterious figure who so nicely buried the machete in the ground. I told him we left it there to be found properly with a search warrant. He was smiling from ear to ear.

"The only problem is, we can't identify the figure who buried it, too dark to see. But that's beside the point. Fingerprints on the machete should reveal the killer," I said.

Lincoln thanked me and got on the phone to the D.A.'s office to get a search warrant, using me as cause. He said that I suspected Doan through my investigation as a blackmail victim, and about the connection to the machete that murdered Noreen and the machete Doan kept from the commercial. He told the D.A. that he wanted Judge Mortimore to be the one to issue the warrant. He smiled and hung up.

Not more than a half hour had gone by when Lincoln's phone rang, and he had his warrant. Judge Mortimore was more than happy to give out a warrant for this case. I could imagine why.

Lincoln gathered a team of officers, had a briefing, then they all headed out. He stopped me and said I could come to watch, but had to stay back. I agreed.

I drove up to Doan's and followed four cars into the lot. Eight officers streamed out and into the building. Three went around the back with metal detectors. Earlier I had told Lincoln where the stick was, and he told the cops doing the search. I watched from the parking lot as they found the spot and dug it up. They took out the newspaper wrapped weapon, and Lincoln went over to examine it. They had a CSI unit come in to take the machete to examine it. People were herded out of the building, Doan was taken in for questioning, and the rest of the employees were questioned and released.

Lincoln smiled at me as he passed by on his way to his car. I drove up to Buck's and found him out walking around his backyard with the metal detector. I had to laugh. He looked up and saw me. He shut down the thing after stabbing the spot he stopped at with the probe. He came over to where I was sitting on his picnic table.

"Jimmy, did you catch your murderer?" he asked as he set the detector on the table.

"Well, they got the weapon now. Just have to get some prints off it to catch the killer." We talked a bit, then I told him I was heading down to watch the interrogation of Doan, I'd talk more to him later. I went off, got to Roseville, and headed towards Lincoln's office. He was walking down a hall and saw me.

"We had the lab do double time on the weapon. We got him. Want to see the interrogation?" he asked.

"I'd love to," I replied. We went to the observation room, and I went in. The same suit was in there. He smiled, and I asked if he was assigned to this precinct. He laughed and said they sent him to take care of the minor cases. I looked at him and asked if he knew what the implications were here? He said it was a murder case of a Dominatrix, hardly a big case. I chuckled and said, "This involved big name politicians and an assortment of celebrities all using this Dom. Take a look at the man in the hot seat. He's Albert Doan, of Doan Appliances, a customer of the murdered Dom and owner of one of the biggest chains of appliance stores in Midwestern America. Tell me that's not important?"

He straightened, went to the window and looked. "Oh, yeah, I've seen his commercials. Wow, he's a killer?"

"For the police to determine and your office to prosecute. You are new around here?" I asked.

"Well, yes, I've been with this D.A.'s office for about five months. So I am fairly new," he defended.

"OK, uh, what's your name?"

"Leo Politano. You are Jim Richards. It's on the warrant. You were the cause for it," he said.

"I'm honored. So, Leo, what's your take on all this?"

"I don't know. I was assigned to this about an hour ago. I'm here to observe and report to my superiors."

"OK, works for me, I guess." Lincoln walked into the interrogation along with Gregory. I was a bit amazed Lincoln would share the questioning, but maybe good cop, bad cop.

"Let the inquisition begin," I said.

Through the speakers, Lincoln's voice came out clearly, "Mr. Doan, you have been read your rights, correct?"

Doan sat quietly, and then nodded his head. Lincoln yelled, "Come on, Doan, let's talk up so we can hear you!" and pounded on the table. Doan jumped.

Gregory put a hand on Lincoln's shoulder and said, "Benny, calm down."

Dominatrix Murders

Oh, I could see who the good cop was now. I was going to love this show.

Lincoln sat back fuming, staring down Doan. Gregory spoke now. "Mr. Doan, we have the machete used in the murder of Noreen Weston, aka Noreen Black. Your prints were all over the weapon, and bloodstains match Noreen. We got you. We just want to know why. Come on, Doan, talk to us."

Doan sat silent. Lincoln jumped up and pounded on the table with both hands. "Talk, Doan or I swear, you will regret it!" He snarled and put his face up to Doan. He would scare me in that position. Doan flinched and looked with terror at Lincoln.

"I didn't do it! I was at a party with the Mayor of Warren that night," he cried.

Lincoln growled, "We did a check on that, Doan. Everyone says you were missing for about an hour and a half that night. People were looking for you, but couldn't find you. Some people say you came back in a different suit. What, you got blood on the first one and had to change? Huh, Doan?"

Lincoln was spitting mad. Gregory pulled him back to his seat and looked at Doan. "Come on, talk to us, Doan. It looks bad for you."

"I didn't do it," he repeated.

Gregory leaned in. "Doan, we have the machete that killed Noreen Weston. It has her blood on it. We have your prints all over the thing, only yours, explain that to me if you didn't do it."

"Someone is framing me," he said quietly.

Lincoln exploded and stomped around the room. "Framing you! Framing you! That's a weak excuse, Doan." Lincoln picked up a chair and threw it against a wall.

Doan covered his head and started crying. He put his head on the table and cried like a baby. Lincoln stopped and just stared at Doan. He looked at Gregory and sat. They both were silent as Doan blubbered.

Lincoln slapped his hand on the table startling Doan upright. His eyes were bloodshot now and tears streamed down his cheeks. Gregory moved forward and said, "Why, Doan, why would someone want to frame you? For your money, fame? None of that will do any good if you're convicted of murder. No one would benefit from framing you."

"Revenge," Doan said. "They wanted to get revenge on me by framing me."

"OK, good choice, now who wanted revenge on you? An employee, a competitor...your wife?"

Doan looked incensed when Gregory suggested his wife. He came up out of the chair and reached out for Gregory with both hands, but Lincoln bashed him back. Doan went slamming into the wall, and Gregory went around to him and held him down, Doan still flailing his arms around. They both had to subdue him.

I thought Gregory had hit a sore spot on that one.

*

Chapter Thirty

They gathered Doan up and took him out of interrogation. I walked out of observation to see them cuff him and hand Doan over to a couple uniformed cops who took him back to his cell. Gregory walked by me with a big grin, took a pretend shot at me with his finger and winked. Lincoln came up and smiled. I followed him to his squad room where he stopped to get some coffee out of the coffee maker.

"I love the routine you guys pulled. It was so professional, so realistic." I grinned.

"I wanted to play the good cop, but everyone knows I do better as the bad cop." He took me to his cubbyhole and said they were going to have Doan arraigned on murder one that afternoon. He sat, and I stood by the desk. I said I was glad this all worked out.

"Where are you going to spend your retirement now that this is over?" I asked.

"The wife and I have a house up in Houghton Lake, had it for years as a retirement home. We may move there to get away from this crappy town."

I said, "Well, I wish you all the best. Despite your rep, I think you're the good guy." I shook his hand and went out of his office to my car. I thought better in my car, so I sat there for a minute, going over what had happened, then drove out.

I got to my office, stood just outside the door looking at the lobby chairs and sighed. I was already missing the anticipation of some sexy female coming through. Oh, well. I entered my office and put the metal detector from my car into the ample closet. I went and sat at my desk, feeling a little drained. I guess it was the crash I would feel when cases were closed. Ralph was going to trial tomorrow, and Doan would follow shortly after. My job was finished.

Dominatrix Murders

Still, I thought about Doan and why would he keep denying killing Noreen when the evidence was so stacked up. They had his fingerprints on the machete and her blood on the thing. What good would it do to keep saying he didn't do it? Could someone be framing him? Why? What did he do to deserve that? Why did Gregory's mention of his wife send him off the edge like that? Who was the dark figure in the garden burying the machete, and now that I thought about it, why bury it back there when a dumpster would do just as good for disposal? Could someone be setting him up and left the machete there to be found? Damn, I was starting to wonder if Doan really was the murderer. Lincoln wouldn't be happy if he wasn't the killer and we got the wrong person. I had to stop thinking like that. They got Doan hands down, but my mind just kept running through possibilities. I needed something to take my mind off the subject.

I putzed around the office for about an hour waiting for a new case to pop in my door, feeling a bit lonely. I called Trapper. I didn't want to bother him, but I wanted to tell him about the interrogation. Trapper was out on a call, so I said I'd call back.

I opened my desk drawer and realized I still had my two checks from Elma and Benson. I signed the backs, drove over to my bank and deposited them, keeping out a little pocket money. I had enough from the two cases to live nicely for a month, but didn't want to blow it too fast. I went to get a bite to eat and decided to go with my second favorite food, Burger King. I was sitting in the restaurant eating when my cell phone rang. It was Trapper. He said he heard I called and asked how the interrogation with Doan went. I filled him in on the details. I could tell he was loving every word. He really didn't like Doan. I said I might go watch the trial of Ralph tomorrow since I had nothing better to do now. He said he would like to come but he was on a new homicide case that would keep him busy for a while, but he would keep in contact. He hung up, and I finished my lunch, went back to my office, and took a nap on the couch I put there for just such events as naps. It's a bitch getting old.

Buck called, awakening me from my dream of hookers dancing around my office. He asked what I was doing. I said nothing much, and he said they called for Elma to come in to testify today. I said I thought the trial didn't start till tomorrow, but he said they moved it up a day. I said I'd come out to get him, and we could pick up Elma on the way. Buck said he would call Elma to let her know we were on the way. Just as I was going out, I found a man standing at my door, startling me. He asked if I was Jim Richards. I said I was, hoping for a client. He handed me a paper and said I was summoned to court, and he left. I looked at the paper. It was for Ralph's trial. I was called in as a witness. I was surprised that they would do something on such short notice, but since I was going there anyway, it didn't matter.

Dominatrix Murders

I drove out and got Buck. He insisted on driving his van. We went to get Elma and headed to Pontiac. On the way I called Benson, and he explained that the court docket was so bogged down, since the jury was already selected that morning, the judge decided to go to trial that afternoon. I told him we were almost there, and he said he would meet us at the front door to the courthouse to get us in without going through the line to be searched. He asked if I had my gun, and I said I did. He asked if I could leave it in the car. I agreed.

We got there, and after we parked Benson met us and took us through to the court room. The judge was just entering, and we did the little up and down for him. Ralph was already at the defendant's table and looking sullen. The trial started, and we endured the opening remarks which were basically a waste of time since Ralph confessed and there were witnesses to his deed. The thing went on for about two hours, and I was called to explain my part. The video was played, and the pictures at the B&D club were shown. Elma was called and testified to her part in the murder. She held up and didn't swear once when she referred to her soon to be ex-husband. Benson was called and testified that Ralph confessed to stabbing the Dominatrix and his two previous wives, both on my recording and in the police interrogation. A couple of other people were called in regard to the murder of his previous two wives, their testimony going to Ralph's mental state. The whole thing ran so quickly, I thought it was a TV show—you know, solve the thing in under an hour, complete with commercials.

Both sides rested their cases, so the jury was given their instructions and taken away to deliberate their verdict. Buck, Elma, Benson and I went out to the lobby and sat talking small talk. About a half hour later the court bailiff came out to Benson and said the jury was back. Benson looked surprised, and we went in. The jury filed back in, the judge read the paper and handed it back to the bailiff. He handed it to the jury foreman, who was asked for their verdict. It was guilty! Murder one. I could see Elma breathe out with the verdict. Ralph was sent back to his cell for sentencing tomorrow morning at 9:30. We stood around outside the courthouse and talked about the trial for a while then we said our good-byes to Benson and went to Buck's van. We dropped Elma off at her home and asked if she wanted to go to the sentencing tomorrow. She did.

Buck drove back to his place, and we sat in the backyard talking about the events of the last week and how it all went by so fast. We laughed at our adventures at the B&D club and the expression on Buck's face when the Dom started in on Ralph. I said I wished I had taken a picture of him for my scrapbook. He said he wasn't very photogenic and probably would have broken the camera. We talked about the trial and how well Elma held up. Buck asked what I was going to do now that my cases were finished. I said I was going to go into my office and play a bunch of Sudoku games on my Palm until a new case came up. He said to let him know if I needed his help, especially if it involved sex clubs. I said that I would. He reminded me that Penny and I promised to take him to a strip club. I said we would be sure to do that. I left him, went back to my office and back to the couch to continue that dream of the dancing girls.

*

Chapter Thirty-one

I didn't mind my phone ringing. It was usually important, but when it interrupted my dreams of sexy women, it was just annoying. I answered after checking the caller I.D. It said *private*. I said hello. It was Lincoln. He asked me to come over to the precinct, there was a small problem. I got myself together, went there and into the squad room where Lincoln was. He and Gregory were standing and talking. They saw me, and I went to them.

"Jim, you saw a person bury the weapon that night, right?" Gregory asked.

"Yeah, it was too dark to see who it was," I replied.

"Could you tell from the person's body type or movements if it was a male or possibly a female?"

I thought for a moment. I looked at them and said, "Well, it didn't move like a 50-some year old man. The person did move a little smoother and with a form that might have been a woman. Still, it was really hard to tell. But it could have been a woman. Why?"

"Mrs. Doan came in an hour ago and claims she was the one who murdered Weston. We let her sit in interrogation to think about it." Lincoln scowled. "We just wanted to get your take on the night visitor who buried the weapon."

"After I left earlier, I was starting to wonder why would Doan sneak in and hide the thing on his property when he could have dumped it anywhere. I don't think he had that much of an attachment to it," I offered.

"Yeah, had me thinking, too," Lincoln said.

Gregory looked at Lincoln and said, "You want to be the good guy this time?" Lincoln smiled and said he enjoyed being a prick. They headed to interrogation, saying I could watch.

I went in and found Mr. Suit again, nodded to him. Gregory and Lincoln went in and sat across from Doan's wife. They asked if she was read her rights. She said yes. They told her the session was being recorded on video, was that all right with her? She said it was. Then they asked if she needed an attorney, she said no.

"For the record, state your name," Gregory requested.

"Beverly Jane Doan," she said.

"You are the wife of the accused murderer, Albert Doan?"

"Yes, I am, but he didn't do it. I did," she said.

"OK, tell us why we should believe you when we have hard proof that your husband did do it."

She was silent for a moment, then she said, "I found out my husband was going to a Dominatrix. It pissed me off." She paused. "I'll start at the beginning. One day two weeks ago there was a phone call for Albert. He wasn't home. I asked the person if there was a message, and he said that they wanted the cash tomorrow at the drop off point or else they would tell the newspapers about his little fetish. I asked him what he was talking about. He laughed and said to ask my husband. Then he hung up. Albert came home, and I asked him about it. He tried to tell me to forget it. We got into an argument, and he finally told me he was seeing a Dominatrix and was being blackmailed by her not to tell. I was shocked. I couldn't believe my husband would do such a thing." She paused, cleared her throat.

Lincoln asked if she would like some water. She said that would be nice. He got it for her from the cooler in the room and handed it to her in a paper cup.

She drank, then continued, "We really got into a screaming match. I was worried about our standing in the community if this got out, and what would happen to his business. I wasn't thinking about his problems, just my own. I badgered him about who this tart was, and he finally told me. I said we have to do something about it, to stop it. He said there was nothing to do but pay them. I said for how long, till we were broke? He stormed out and didn't come back till late." She paused again for a drink of water.

"We had the Warren Mayor's party to go to the next night. I said I wasn't feeling well and he should go by himself. He was still mad about our fight and said that was fine with him. He got ready and left. I was still pissed and saw that stupid knife of his hanging on the wall. I took it down, wearing gloves, and put it in an oversized purse I had. I looked up this Dominatrix's address and went there. It was her office, but she wasn't there, just some blond girl at a desk. I pretended to be an old friend of Noreen in town for a visit and wanted to surprise her. The dumb bitch gave me her home address. She should be fired."

Dominatrix Murders

I smiled at that remark, knowing Melody was in jail.

"I went to her house and sat outside for a while. Finally a woman drove up and went in the house. I went to the door, rang the bell, and she answered. I asked if she was Noreen Black. She was hesitant, but said yes. I pulled the machete out and pointed it at her. She was shocked to see what I had and backed away, then she turned to run but I started hacking at her, just swinging the thing until she fell, and then I continued to hack. Finally I severed her head."

Lincoln asked what she did with the head.

"I put it on a shelf in the living room next to a cute picture of her family. I called Albert at his party and told him what I had done. He was in a panic and said he was coming to get me. I said I was going home and hung up. I put the machete back in my bag and left. I got back home and was cleaning up just as Albert arrived. He grabbed on to me and shook me, yelling about what I had done. I was still covered in blood, and got some on him. He said he was finished with me, and we would discuss this later. He changed his jacket and went out. I found out later he went back to his precious party and enjoyed himself. He came back, packed a bag, and said he was going to a motel. He was gone for a week. I just stayed around the house getting madder and madder. I took the machete and buried it in his flower bed out back of his office. I was going to call the police anonymously and tell them it was there, but you beat me to it." She smiled and drank some water.

"Why are you coming forward now?" Lincoln asked.

"I wanted him to know the humiliation of being pulled into a jail and treated like a criminal."

"Why didn't you wait for him to go to trial and be sentenced, then come forward?" Lincoln asked.

"Because I'm going to die today. I just wanted to make him suffer before I go. Oh, I don't want him in prison for what I did. I'm not that cruel. I'm not happy with what I did to that woman. It's been eating at me, and so I must atone for my sins. That's why I'm here to confess and die," she said with a smile.

"How do you know you're going to die today?" Gregory asked.

"Because I'm going to kill myself," she reached into a small pocket of her billowing dress, pulled out a small caliber pistol, held it in her mouth, and pulled the trigger. The back of her head exploded as Gregory and Lincoln jumped up. Gregory ran to the door yelling to call for EMTs. Lincoln went to her and saw that she was gone. He told Gregory.

Dominatrix Murders

We all were in shock. I looked over to the suit. He was vomiting in the corner.

I came out of observation. Lincoln came out, looked at me, and said, "I'm definitely retiring now."

After Mrs. Doan's body was taken out and the room was being cleaned, Lincoln and I sat on chairs in the squad room. I asked, "Do you believe she did it?"

"Oh, I know she did. You see, the head was put on a shelf in the living room, and we never let that detail out. She had to have done it. I'll ask Doan if he can tell me what he did with the head just to be sure, but I'm good for her doing it."

"You don't need me anymore today?" I asked.

"I won't need you at all now that this case is officially closed. You did good, Richards. I didn't like you at first, but you're all right," he said quietly.

I stood and said, "Well, you're all right, too. I'm getting out of here. Enjoy your retirement."

*

Chapter Thirty-two

He smiled, and I left. I got back to my office and called Weston and told him to come to my office as soon as he could, I had some news for him. He said he'd be right over. About a half hour later he came in, and I asked him to sit. I told him about the events of the last couple of days and that we found Noreen's murderer. I told him who and why all the way back to Marylou in the bar, to Melody and Bruce, finally up to Doan and his wife.

Weston was quiet. "All because two nitwits wanted to blackmail a few people. Damn stupid. Well, thank you, Mr. Richards. I'll have a check to you soon as possible."

"Don't worry about it. Put the cash towards your children, just a little gift from me," I said as we walked to the door.

He said he was going up to Port Huron to visit them, and he would buy something special for them. I asked for the address or number in Port Huron in case I needed to get in touch with him. He pulled out a Palm Zire 72 and turned it on to get the number. I was amazed someone besides me used a Palm. I asked him how long he had it. He said it was actually his wife's, he got it after she was murdered. He didn't know much about how the thing worked, just the address book. I felt a skip of my heartbeat and asked him if I could see it.

I showed him my Palm and took his to my desk. He followed. I cycled through the pages and found a file that said "Clients." I was feeling real good right then. I opened the file, and it was a list of names, codes and links to other information in the file. A database of her clients. I asked if he minded if I copied the file to my Palm. He said he didn't care. I did a beam process that sent the file to my Palm TX by wireless link. I checked the file on my Palm and then deleted the file on his. I told him not to say anything to anyone else about the Palm or the file I just copied, it could be dangerous for him or his family. He said he didn't want to know, gave me the number where he was going to be and left.

Finally found what everyone was looking for, the list. I sat back and grinned from ear to ear as I read off names.

I cycled through the names on the list and found an interesting entry. It was a Dora Lincoln. Now why did that name pique my interest? I called Lincoln, and he finally came on. I told him that I found Noreen's client list. He was silent.

"I found it on a computer," I lied. "All the names, numbers and personal information of her clients." Still no reaction from Lincoln. "Is your wife's name

Dora?" I asked and he quietly said no, that was his sister.

"Well, anyway, I deleted the file on the computer, too dangerous to leave lying around, but not before I rummaged through it. So I just wanted to let you know the list is now history." I heard him say thank you. I said, you're welcome, and hung up. I thought Lincoln would rest easier that night. I put a copy of the file on an SD card and put it in my lock box. Might be handy one day.

I was totally ripped, so I headed home and found Penny sitting on the couch watching a sad movie. She was tearing up with used tissues all around her. I sat next to her and asked if this was a hormonal thing that she discussed on her show. She smacked my arm and said to shut up, she was watching her movie. When it ended, I told her about my day. She smiled and said I did good. I was feeling good. So I took her out to a fancy sit down dinner at a real restaurant, and we had some wine. Then we got home and had some beer and crawled into bed to watch a happy movie.

The next morning, Penny and I were getting ready to go out, she to play host, and I to watch Ralph get his just desserts. Penny stopped me at the kitchen. She looked worried.

"What's the matter?" I asked.

"Don't go out today, stay home for me," she said quietly.

"Why?"

"It's silly, I know, but I had a bad dream. In it you got shot." She was grabbing my shirt like she was not going to let me go.

"Penny, I'm not going to get shot. Don't worry. I'm just going to a courtroom to watch Ralph Flagg get sentenced. I'm sure I won't get shot in a courthouse. Now go to work and don't worry about me," I said to comfort her.

She looked at me, gave me a big kiss and went off. I stood at the door thinking about what she said.

A half hour later I was in Trapper's office waiting for him to go to Pontiac with me. He looked at me and asked if I was all right, I had a strange look on my face. I said that I didn't think it was anything.

An hour later we met Buck in front of the courthouse. He had Elma with him. We all went in. Lawson was at the entrance and led us around the line to be searched for explosive devices. He signaled to a guard that we were good, and we went into the courtroom.

Ralph was seated at his table, and we sat about three rows back. They had what amounted to church pews for seating, and we sat with Elma on the aisle. She was avoiding looking at Ralph. The judge came in, and we stood and sat for his honor. He looked at the papers in front of him and told Ralph to stand. He did, along with his lawyer. The judged passed a life sentence on Ralph for the murder of the dominatrix. The court was making little noises and the judge banged his gavel demanding silence. The judge told the officer to take Ralph to a holding cell for transfer to county lock-up. The guard came over and started to take Ralph's arm when Ralph tackled the guard. They went down, and when Ralph came back up off the floor, he had the guard's gun. He fired once into the ceiling, and everyone ducked down. He jumped forward, grabbed Elma, and dragged her towards the front doors, putting an arm around her neck. Trapper, Lawson and I moved out from the pews and had our guns out.

Ralph had the strangle hold on Elma with his left arm and swung the gun back and forth at Trapper, Lawson and me. We had our guns aimed at him but didn't want to hit Elma. Ralph looked at me, and I could see hatred in his eyes.

"This is all your fault, Richards, you and your damn interference." He pointed his gun at me and fired twice, hitting me in the chest. I fell back. Elma screamed and stomped on Ralph's foot then bit the wrist around her neck. He screamed and pulled his arm away, just enough for Elma to get loose. As soon as she was clear, shots rang out from Trapper and Lawson, dropping Ralph like a brick, blood streaming from the holes in his chest.

Buck ran to me, yelling for a doctor. "Jimmy, don't die, man. You can't die! Where's a fucking medic?"

Trapper was laughing as he came towards Buck and me. Buck looked up and yelled, "What's the matter with you? Get help for Jim!"

Buck fell back when I yelled at him to get off my chest. His eyes went wide, and he was speechless as I sat up. Trapper helped me to my feet, and Buck sprang up.

"What the hell, Jim, you aren't hurt?" I pulled open my shirt to reveal a bulletproof vest. Buck said, "What the hell?"

Trapper asked me, "Just how did you know to ask me for the damn thing? How could you know that you would get shot at?"

I looked at both of them and said, "Penny had a dream I was going to get shot so I was being cautious."

"Well, score one big one for Penny." Trapper cheered. I pulled the bullets out of the vest and said I had two more things to put on my office wall. I looked over at Ralph on the floor now being covered by the bailiffs as they cleared the courtroom.

Elma came rushing over and hugged me, saying, "I thought Ralph killed you!"

"Elma, you did real good getting away from Ralph," Trapper said.

She looked at the covered body of Ralph and said, "Looks like I won't need a divorce now." We all laughed.

About an hour after all the excitement died, everyone was heading out. I thanked Buck for his concern and Trapper for the vest. He told me to keep it, but don't say anything about it. I said I'd treasure it. I got to my car. My chest was starting to hurt a bit less than when I was first hit. I put the vest on the front seat next to me and drove back home.

I got to the front door, and Penny flung it open, saying I wasn't shot. I pulled her to me and gave her a good tonsil search. She looked at me and asked what brought that on.

"Hold out your hand," I said, and dropped the two bullets onto her palm. She looked at them and asked, what were they for?

"I'll never doubt your dreams again." I took her to the couch and explained what had happened that day and how after she told me that morning about her dream, I borrowed a Kevlar vest from Trapper just as a precaution. Lucky I did. She was tearing up and grabbed on to me. I kissed her cheek and was thankful for her.

THE END

*For every ending,
there is a new beginning.*

~~*~~

The following is a preview of the 4th book, "Mistress Murders".

Chapter One

My chest was still sore from the two bullets I took at the courthouse during Ralph Flagg's sentencing. Bulletproof Kevlar vests may protect you from having a bullet rip through your body, but not from the impact, it hurts. Take my word for it, I was hit in the chest twice now, once in Vegas and now here in Michigan. My poor little

Palm Treo cell phone stopped the bullet in the Vegas desert, it wasn't a Kevlar vest, but it prevented me from dying. The two bullets from the courthouse, that the Kevlar stopped, were now part of a plaque on my wall, next to the plaque with the bullet and cell phone from the Vegas shooting. I expected more plaques on the wall, not because I liked to get shot, just having them there meant I wasn't killed.

I sat in my office, devoid of clients, playing Sudoku on my Palm TX for the millionth time and wondering if this was all worth it. I had been almost killed three times and because of my investigations, the love of my life, Penny, had come close to harm also. I put the Palm down and looked at my door, still lacking the flashing lights I thought about putting around it, to make it look more like Las Vegas. I was wondering how Deacon and Lynn were getting along in Vegas, I hadn't heard from them in a while. Deacon looked so cute following after Lynn, when we met her investigating the showgirl murders. Like a puppy in love.

I was thinking about going to the computer on my desk to play Mah Jong tiles, when my door opened, startling me. I half expected either Trapper or Buck, but the person who did come in was a welcome sight, a gorgeous red-head. I figured she was a left over from the now closed call girl business upstairs, she just hadn't heard that the police shut it down yet.

"Mr, Richards?" she said in a silky smooth voice, very slightly nasal, but dreamy.

"Yes, may I help you?" I replied, standing up.

"I need your services," she asked.

"Please, come in, would you like some coffee?" I asked, she said no. I continued, "Well then, tell me what it is you need exactly."

She went to the client chair as I pointed it out, we both sat, she crossed her slim, attractive legs. Her beautiful face had a distressed look now, sad, yet she looked somewhat irritated.

"I'm in need of having my husband watched to see what it is he does during the times he's not with me," she said.

"You want him followed to see if he is cheating on you?" I asked.

"Well, yes, I guess I do suspect him of cheating, but mostly to see what he is up to. I suspect he maybe planning on divorcing me and I want to be prepared. Do you understand?"

"Oh, yes, get the jump on him and his holdings," I mused.

"Then you do understand," she said with a coy little smile.

"Quite clearly now, I'll need some information on him," I said as I handed her my rate card, "These are my fees, you decide how much you want and I'll go from there."

She studied the card for a moment then said the full treatment would be fine, she wanted all information on him. She opened her purse, took out two hundred dollars in fifties, and handed them to me for the advance, then I handed her a pad and pencil.

"Would you please write down any information about him to help me get a feel for his movements or activities. List places he goes, where he works, any habits he may have, favorite drinking hole, maybe a few friends and where I can find them. I'll also need to know where he banks, the ones you know of, and names of any lawyers he may have." I said.

She busied herself writing a book, then handed it to me. I saw his name was David Paul. I asked if she had a picture of David, she took one out of her purse and handed it to me. He was a very handsome man, I could see women tripping over themselves to get to him.

"Why do you feel David may divorce you, Mrs. Paul?" I asked.

"Please, call me Rene, well, he's been moving little things out of the house, his personal items, books, papers, things like that. Then he took out his jewelry without saying anything. I usually don't check his drawers, but I looked the other day and his jewelry was gone," she said.

"He's removing valuables then?" I asked.

"Yes, like he's preparing for something."

"Could he be pawning the jewelry to pay gambling debts?" I asked.

"David, has never been involved with gambling. We were in Las Vegas for a week and he never once went in the casinos to gamble. He doesn't trust games of chance. Too risky he says."

"OK, on the subject of cheating, does he show signs of having a mistress?" I asked.

"He has changed a bit in that respect, the way he's happy all the time, not like he was a few months ago. He's different, and spending more time away from home, staying late for work, things like that." She took a hanky from her purse and dabbed her eyes.

"Mrs. Paul, you're a very beautiful woman, why would he want to divorce you?"

"Thank you, Mr. Richards, but beauty isn't always something a man can hold on to, a healthy relationship is important, too. I thought we had one, but it seems he wants more."

"Do you think he may be planning a divorce to be with this other woman, if there is another woman?"

"I was hoping you could tell me that," she said quietly.

"Of course, I'll be checking on him as soon as possible, and give you my reports," I said.

She stood and said, "Thank you, Mr. Richards, I'll be waiting to hear from you."

I gave her my business card and said to call me if anything occurs that may help. She said she would and left.

I sat back and read the pad she wrote her husband's info on. He had a busy life; work, he was an account executive for a major bank, and he loved sports. He was a huge Detroit Tigers fan, had season box seat tickets. Never missed a game when he could attend. He drove a Cadillac CTS and owned a boat. Loved to fish and went out most weekends to Lake St. Clair. He belonged to a gym, went three times a week. When did he find time for his gorgeous wife? Shame really, she was a knockout. But as she said, looks aren't everything. I stared at his picture, getting his face in my head so I could identify him later. Could Davey boy be fooling around?

My door opened again and in walked a matronly woman, probably in her late fifties, but youthful looking. She was well dressed, had money by her demeanor and she was leading a dog on a leash.

"Are you the detective?" she asked with an air of snootiness.

"Last time I looked at my license, I was."

She just looked at me, scrunched up her face and said, "Are you serious?"

"I can be, what can I do for you?"

"I'm Mrs. Elizabeth Truedell, I need protection, a bodyguard if you will. Do you provide that service?"

I thought of Buck and said, "Well, Mrs. Truedell, we have in the past, yes. Is this for yourself?"

"Oh goodness, no. This is for Mr. Bennington of Sydney," she said like I knew the guy.

"Is this Mr. Bennington able to come in so I can talk to him?" I inquired.

"Mr. Richards, you can't talk to him, he's my dog," she said, seeming to be annoyed.

I looked down at what I recognized as a Terrier breed, acting as snooty as his master. I suddenly realized the dog had on clothes, a small jacket, making him look dorky. I told her to have a seat and tell me more.

She sat and continued, "Mr. Bennington is an Australian Terrier, and he is a show dog of careful breeding and training. I need to have him watched carefully, there are person's who would like to see my Mr. Bennington not make it to the AKC dog show next week. I've had threats already, they started this week."

"How did you receive the threats?"

"By phone, a gruff voice said it would be a good idea to stay away from the show, or else," she said.

"Or else what," I asked.

"He didn't say, he just hung up after that." The dog sat up for her as her hand went to him. She scratched his ears and patted his head. "So can you provide Mr. Bennington with protection?'

I tried not to laugh and said, "I'm sure we can, I'll talk to my associate and see what kind of schedule we can set-up. I'll need more information from you." I handed her the pad and pencil and asked her to put down names, addresses and dates of the show, along with anything else I should know.

While she was doing that, I looked at the dog, he just took a crap on my carpet.

Continued in the book...

Jim Richards Family of Readers

Thanks to the following people who are now part of the Jim Richards Family of Readers. They have read a book or more and enjoyed them. They all volunteered to be included in the list. If you are a fan of the books, send me your full name and you will be included in future books. Send your name to murdernovels@bobmoats.com to be added here and on the website. (updated 03-23-14)

* Achim Feifel * Al Norris * Alex Wheatley * Alexandra Delporte-Wilkinson * Amy Tapia * Andrea Bryan * Anne Shepherd * Arianda Sugar * Arlene Markowski * Ashley Augustus * Audra Hall * Barbara Hughes * Barbara Sammons * Barbara Schuler * Barbara Zirger * Beth Donohue Plenskofski * Betsy Childress * Beth Gibson * Bill Sandy * Bill Tornquist * Billie-jo Collie * Boni J Rychener * Carl Bishopric * Carla Lewis * Carole Henderson * Carolyn

Bob Moats

Conroy * Carolyn Riddle-Linington * Cassy Bailey * Chad Hudson * Charlotte L Duran * Cheryl L. Everett * Cindy Ackley Nunn * Cindy Valstad * Connie Bancroft * Corinne Kay O'Daniel * Dana Robbins Chuchran * Dana Wichita * Danielle Monique * Darren Heald * Dave Travers * David Wilkinson * DeAnn Jannereth * Deanna Miller * Deb Breuker Balbo * Debbie Carter * Debbie White * Deborah Fartuch * Deborah Gauze * Deborah Sullivan * Dee King * Denise Freeman * Diana Carver * Dixie Beck * Donna Gould * Donna Thompson * Donny Minter * Doris Kight * Eddie Moore * Eric Walters * Felicia Annette Bradfield * Francine Menor * Gail Chesney * Georgiann Minster * George Conner * Greg Colucci * Hayley Rankin * Harold Garcia * Heidi Arnold * Irma Ranee Coy * Jacqueline Moss * Jan Kimball * Janice Schneider * Janice Spoor * Jennifer Redmond * Jessica Keown-Belous * Jim Beck * Jo Boguslaw * Jo Turner * Joanne Marie Turner * John Peiffer * John Wisbiski * Joseph Wauro * Joyce Stacy * Joyce Trifiletti * Judy Franklin * Judy Travers * Judy Padgett * Julie Heath * Junnahvee Benson * Karen Dahl * Karen Grams * Karen Higham * Karen Kaiser * Karen Meinburg Richwine * Karen Kirkman Parker * Karin Hawkins * Karin Vasvari * Kathleen Donohue Roesing * Kathleen Riddle-Wolfe * Kathy Hinds Moore * Kathy Jones * Kathy Mitchell * Katie Benzler * Kay Burns * Kelly Garcia * Ken Boggs * Keota Rodriguez * Kiera Mccarthy * Kim Estes * Kitty Stolle * Kristie Sciler * Kirsty Stanton * LaLonnie Scallen * Larry Morris * Leann Parr * Lenora Scales * Leslie Marie Jackson * Linda Forester * Linda Ingle Cox * Linda Kennerö * Linda Magill * Lisa Bower * Liz Gibson * Lorraine Wiman * Loretta Alexander * Lynda Bowles * Lynette Lawrance * LuAnn Louttit * Manny Rothman * Marcia Gibson DeWitt * Marie Calder * Marlene Bryan * MaryLouise Kramp * Mary Lynn Gross * Megan Atkins * Meghan Hyden * Melody Cannavan * Michael Carruthers * Michael Dinkens * Michael Vannoy * Michelle Burns-

Dominatrix Murders

Mitchell * Michelle Pilcher * Micki Potter * Mike Moats * Mimi Baur * Myrna Hecht * Nadine Sutton * Natalie Quine * Neena Martin * O'Della Wilson * Pat Pollington * Pat Rohn * Patricia Jarmon * Patricia C Trezza * Patrick Barry * Paul Lawrance * Peggy Davis * Phyllis Bassett * Raylene Matheny * Rebecca Collins Besner * Renee Brumley * Reta Hanna * Reta Moats * Roberta Navarro-Harder * Sally Berneathy * Sally Hubler * Sarah Santos * Satka Nikc * Sharon E. Edwards * Sharon Mangini * Sharon McMillon * Sheena Rawl * Sherry Amstutz * Shirley Alvarez * Shirley Davies * Shirley Williams * Stacie Rowe * Stephanie Conner * Steve Cullen * Susan Haughton * Susan Hesse Adams * Susan Salomon * Suzan K Chase * Taisha Cullum * Tamara Moore * Tammy Castleberry * Tammy Lynn Wood * Ted Murphy * Terri Atkins * Terri Creech * Terry Raab * Tonia Rachael Riggs-Williams * Travis Fleury-Lopez * Twyla Gawlas * Val Brooks * Walt Munsel * Yvonne Isakson *

Thank you to all these wonderful people.

Thank you for purchasing this book. I hope you enjoy it as much as I enjoyed writing it for my faithful readers. Please feel free to email me to tell me what you thought about my stories. I love hearing from the readers. I can be reached at murdernovels@bobmoats.com thanks again!